westland ltd

BY THE WATER COOLER

Parul Sharma is the author of the bestselling novel *Bringing Up Vasu – That First Year*. She lives in Mumbai with her family.

# by the water cooler

### PARUL SHARMA

## westland ltd

Venkat Towers, 165, P.H. Road, Opp. Maduravoyal Municipal Office, Chennai 600 095
No. 38/10 (New No. 5), Raghava Nagar, New Timber Yard Layout, Bangalore 560 026
Survey No. A-9, II Floor, Moula Ali Industrial Area, Moula Ali, Hyderabad 500 040
23/181, Anand Nagar, Nehru Road, Santacruz East, Mumbai 400 055
47, Brij Mohan Road, Daryaganj, New Delhi 110 002

First published by westland ltd 2010

Copyright © Parul Sharma, 2010

10 9 8 7 6 5 4 3 2 1

ISBN: 9789380658377

Typeset by Manju

Printed at Manipal Press Limited

*For Sainath, who took care of the kids, the bills and the world while I wrote.*

# *one*

Tanya was dressed in western formals — a smart jacket-suit, I noticed, as soon as she walked into the conference room. This deviation from the plan and the universally-accepted BFF code did not escape my keen eye, and my thoughts immediately started to run on the lines of — *For thirty pieces of silver, you lying-cheating Judas? We had decided on ethnic chic-dripping salwar-kameezes, and yet here you are, looking smarter than bargained for in that crisp skirt-suit.*

I glowered at her, trying to communicate the words with my eyes. She steadfastly ignored me. I continued to glower for a few more moments till I realised that the other occupant in the room, a newcomer like us, was looking at me nervously, wondering perhaps if he would be required to make a sudden dash for the door if things took a turn for the violent. I immediately rearranged my features into an expression of calm repose. He relaxed visibly. Tanya, meanwhile, was now paying great attention to her (blank) notebook. 'Come and sit next to me,' I hissed at her when she continued to display an acute interest in the wordless pages for a considerable length of time.

'No,' she refused flatly, without looking up.

'Why not?' I asked, when no further explanation was offered.

'Because you look like you're emanating negative vibes,' she said, as if negative vibes were things that real people talked about.

'I will emanate more than just vibes if you don't come and sit next to me,' I threatened and then added a quick glower.

She looked up, sighed loudly, and with a quick apologetic smile at the formerly nervous and now only skinny man who was watching us with a lot of interest, got up and took the chair next to mine.

'Why did you wear a skirt-suit? Now I look like your grandmother,' I wasted no time in getting to the core of the issue.

'My grandmother was a fine woman, I will have you know. Stately and elegant. Perhaps a little podgy around the waist, but that may have been because of her fondness for her besan laddoos,' said Tanya.

'Were they very nice?' I asked, in spite of myself.

'I don't know, they never made it past her. Anyway, so the skirt-suit was a last-minute thing. Seriously, Mini, you look great. That green,' she vaguely gestured at my clothes, 'it brings out the colour of your eyes.' I briefly wondered how green could bring out the black in my eyes but let it pass.

The door opened and a familiar face peeked inside. The face had a set of perfect white teeth shining in it, and was framed by a bunch of tight, black curls. The rest of the body followed this striking face inside. This was John

Peters, the human resource manager who had interviewed both Tanya and me (and presumably the skinny man) for our new positions. A little splash of Kerala in Mumbai, was how Tanya had described him. He was the one who had convinced us that leaving our jobs with the Mumbai office of a high-profile, global advertising agency was a good idea as the move would ensure that our climb up the corporate ladder would be a positive trot. Or jog. Brisk, at any rate.

'Hello, hello, so all three of you are here. Very good, very good. Subbu, have you introduced yourself to the two ladies? They join us in marketing. Subbu will be in accounts,' John Peters performed the introductions.

We exchanged watery smiles with Subbu of accounts. This was a case of perfect casting. Subbu looked like he was itching to get at the accounting files.

John Peters wiped his forehead and then looked at us as if he was seeing us for the first time. Then he seemed to remember who we were. Tanya stifled a giggle. John looked even more nervous. He launched into speech. 'Well, it is my privilege to welcome you to the JR Enterprises... uh ... family. JR Enterprises is a leading player in the world of women's fashion. We are known for our values of innovation and imagination...'

I tuned out at this point. Working in advertising had taken away my faith in words forever, and these days I was given to sprinkling salt in the general direction of those like 'innovation' and 'imagination'. Next to me, Tanya was nodding sagely at John Peters. Subbu looked bored.

'...led ably by our CEO Mr Avinash Singh, we are market leaders...'

I hoped we had done the right thing by moving to this new company. It seemed very different from our madhouse ex-office, even in my first few hours here. Of course, a lot of the easy affability at the agency had been pretence, much like the casual sophistication of this new environment was bound to be.

'...five hundred employees, all working diligently towards achieving the common goal of excellence...'

Two years out of business school had been enough for cynicism to grow and blossom. Maybe this place really was different. The money was certainly better, though giving us a raise was not difficult for any company to achieve. Our employers at the advertising agency had believed that we were all still living at home with our parents and only needed pocket money to buy an occasional ice cream or chocolate. Or peanuts. Tanya was now smiling beatifically at John Peters who was delivering his rehearsed presentation with a lot more panache under her unconditional encouragement.

Tanya had joined this company because she was 'terribly overworked' at the agency. She needed 'personal time', she had declared passionately, something that she never got there. Well, we were childhood friends and, by a strange quirk of fate, had followed the same trajectory through business school and then the corporate world. At the agency, we had shared many a late-night pizza while working on beautifying pitch presentations — a task always reserved for minions such as us — and needed to load our system with empty calories.

It was good to have her by my side in this new environment. Of course, she was a liar and a cheat who did not adhere to promises of wearing salwar-kameezes to work on the first day, but that could be dealt with.

'…and at last, I have something else to share with you. I am quitting this company and this is my last day at work. In fact, the presentation that I just shared with you was the very last bit of work that I have performed here. So I guess I should say welcome and … goodbye.' Clearly, John Peters had taken his Presentation Skills 101 seriously and had saved the best and most shocking bit for last.

'Whoa there, Jaypee,' said Tanya after the first few silent seconds had given way to words of shock and disbelief. 'Why? How? Is everything alright? Most importantly, how come you are leaving so suddenly if this place is so great? I mean, you sure sold it hard during the interview process!'

I looked at her and mouthed the question, 'Jaypee?' She ignored me. There was complete silence in the room for a few moments as each of us processed this new and decidedly disturbing piece of information. John Peters looked miserable and stared vacantly back at us.

'Look here, Mr Peters, sir,' Subbu finally found his voice. 'There is clearly something that is not meeting our eyes, yes? Please tell us what is the issue that lies beneath your resignation?'

I looked for the copy of 'Learn Perfect English in 15 Days or Less' that Subbu was clearly reading from and found none. I realised that this, in fact, was the way he spoke.

'I am sorry, friends,' said John Peters, looking more

distressed by the minute, 'it is a personal issue.'

'Well, we have a right to know,' I said. 'I mean, we don't know another soul in this place and now you are suddenly leaving. Come on, tell us what's happened.'

John Peters sat down in one of the several empty chairs in the conference room. He looked at us uneasily. Tanya poured him a glass of water, which he gulped down gratefully.

'Mini, Subbu, Tanya — that guy, the CEO, he is a *maniac*,' he erupted. 'Today he told me that I was better off jumping from the building than trying to give him coherent monthly reports. He told me I was a splotch on the organisation that we were trying to create. I could have let that pass, but then he compared me to the gunk that collects in the coffee machine every month. That was the last straw! I got fired up and told him that I would leave if he continued to speak to me like this. He told me that I had till the end of the day to wrap up my work and clear out my desk. Oh god! What did I do to deserve this?'

Tanya and I exchanged a worried look. The HR manager was rapidly unravelling in front of our eyes.

'Well, how can he just fire you like this, Jaypee? There must be some policy the company follows, right? Right?'

'There is no policy-sholicy, Tanya,' John said miserably. 'The owners of the place — the Mittal family — have given Avinash Singh complete powers to run the company. He turned it around when it was not doing that well and now they worship the ground he walks on. He is the policy and a wicked one, if you ask me.' He got up then, muttering that he needed to get a lot of work done.

'In that case, boy, you sure told us some lies during the interviews. You said he was "a father figure, a competent leader who looked after his people" — to use your exact words,' Tanya said accusingly. 'I wish we had at least had a video-conference with him, but you said that he did not have the time and that you needed to fill these vacancies quickly. You said that Mr Singh trusted your judgement blindly and that as long as Vivek the marketing manager was happy with us, we would be fine.'

'Vivek was happy but he left last week,' said John, making us draw another collective gasp. Our worry was now making way for horror of the abject kind.

'What will your colleagues and your boss say about this, John?' I asked as all three of us stared at his bleak face.

'I don't know. I won't be the first person who has left this company so suddenly,' he said, and looking like he was ready to burst into copious tears, started to pick up his files while at the same time condemning our collective spirit to a trip to the underside of the carpet.

'Wait! What about us?' I asked. 'Where do we go from here?'

'Well, as it happens,' he said, walking out the door, 'you need to follow the schedule that's been given to you, according to which you need to meet ... uh ... the CEO next. Please proceed to his office, the last cabin at the end of the rope, I mean, corridor.'

I glanced down at the neatly typed itinerary that had been given to us for our first day of induction into the new office.

1. Introduction to JR Enterprises by John Peters
2. Brief interaction with Mr Avinash Singh, CEO
3. Introduction to teams

Somehow I had imagined that the second item on the list would be a cosy chat, accompanied by biscuits and steaming mugs of cocoa. I was mistaken. Or hungry.

We stepped out of the conference room together. John had disappeared down the labyrinth of clinically clean corridors that looked forbidding.

'What will we do now? We have been thrown into rocky and uncharted territory with no captain to guide us,' mourned Subbu poetically.

'The captain is there alright, Subbu baby,' corrected Tanya; 'it's a fellow sailor who has been thrown overboard. Tell me, have you seen *Das Boot*?' Predictably, Subbu hadn't. Tanya launched into an enthusiastic explanation of the film. People passing us by stared at us. I saw a fat girl toddling past and approached her gingerly.

'Excuse me, could you show us the way to the CEO's office?' I asked.

She looked at us with a mix of horror and distaste, as if we had asked her to share a particularly delicious slice of pizza with us. She looked like she liked her pizza unshared. She pointed at a door and walked away. There was a small reception area right outside the door. A very attractive girl sat at the station, sorting out some papers and talking on her phone at the same time. She looked up and I couldn't help noticing that she had dark circles under her eyes. She smiled and raised her eyebrows. I could hear Subbu's heart palpitating under that lovely gaze.

'The CEO has asked us in,' explained Tanya.

She nodded and spoke briefly into the other phone. She then pointed at the door and gave us a small, friendly wave. I knocked.

The door was opened by an affable-looking, smiling man. He asked us in and directed us to some chairs. This wasn't half bad; he looked genial enough for a CEO, I supposed. John Peters didn't know any better, I found myself thinking, instinctively warming to this cheerful man in this bleak world of resigning managers, fat and cheerless ladies and overworked secretaries. Then he spoke.

'I am Prakash. Sir will be with you in a minute,' he said, still smiling. It was then that I noticed the other man, sitting behind an imposing desk a few feet away and now shouting into a phone. This other man resembled a bull that had had a rough day at the ring and was letting off steam by trampling a few dozen innocents under his angry hooves.

'How has your day been so far?' Prakash asked, over the din that the man, presumably Avinash, was creating just a short distance away. Tanya and I couldn't help exchanging another worried glance. Prakash caught the look and still smiling, asked gently, 'John Peters? Did he say anything?'

'Not much,' whispered Tanya, 'just a couple of things about why he needed to leave.'

Prakash nodded and continued to smile.

Avinash Singh was getting louder by the minute. I stole a quick look at him. He was a short and stocky man who seemed to compensate for a towering presence with a terrifying temper. The humble green plants looked out of place in his presence. So did the innocent, tiny porcelain figurines on his desk. A decorative theme befitting this chamber would need human skulls and a nice, smart guillotine.

'... then there is no point to this discussion, Arun,' he finally snapped at the unfortunate person on the other end. 'There is no incentive in this for me. Get back to me if you have a better offer. Otherwise let us continue to meet at the gym and nothing more.'

He banged the phone down and stood up. All three of us stood up automatically.

'Prakash, tell that girl not to forward Arun Mehra's calls in future, provided she can process this much information in that pea-sized brain of hers. Are these the new joinees? Sit!'

Three bottoms met the couch at this command. Prakash languidly took a seat next to the boss and fished out a notebook. What was he, another secretary?

'Well, so I have this talk with all the new people in our team. Tell me, why did you join us?' he bowled the first googly of the day.

We remained silent for a few seconds. Then Subbu spoke.

'I had hoped there would be an opportunity for me to learn more and expand my horizons at this company, Sir.'

'Bullshit,' bellowed Avinash, 'get honest or get out.'

Subbu lost a few grams in weight right there and then. Tanya went next, positioning honesty as the key pillar of her strategy, having identified it as the big man's object of desire.

'It's better money than the agency and, hopefully, better work too.'

'Only people who suck at their work complain about it. As for the money, the laws of demand and supply in the labour market ensure each of us gets what he or she deserves.'

Tanya gulped and looked at me. Prakash was still smiling. I was expected to answer next. I tried to disappear by sheer force of will. Having failed at that, I launched an attempt at an answer.

'I have always admired the brand that has been created by JRE. I hoped that, by being a part of the team that works on it, I can contribute to building and nurturing...'

'Oh fuck off,' was the answer I got for my endeavour. I knew when to shut up and did.

'I know why you are all here,' he continued to boom. 'You are here because you want a piece of the action. Action that I have created. Action that I have worked nights for. Action that I have visualised and executed. You want it, don't you? Huh? HUH? So when you come here and spout inanities like team and brand-building, I know you are full of crap, crap and nothing but crap. I guess I should have taken some time out at the recruitment stage. Now I am stuck with three more cases of crappy recruiting by that crappy John Peters.'

This declaration had a somewhat sobering effect on the gathering. Subbu was cowering in his seat. Tanya looked like she was ready to bring forward cocktail hour by a few hours. I could feel the blood draining from my face.

Avinash stood up.

'I have seen you. I have nothing more to say to you. Everything you do will be reported back to me so watch out. Prakash is here to answer questions, if any.' With that he strode back to the desk. We stood up and started to file out of his room, a sombre trio. The pretty secretary saw our collective fallen expression as we were trooping out and smiled at us.

'That bad, eh?' she whispered.

We nodded.

'Well, you won't have to see him everyday,' she said, 'unlike some of us.'

We smiled wryly at her. Then I thought of something that I could ask her.

'Hey, do you think you can help us? We are supposed to meet our respective teams next but since John is ... err ... indisposed, I was wondering if you could help us out.'

'Sure, no problem. Go back to the conference room where you were sitting in the morning and I will speak to Prakash.'

The glum party made its way back to the conference room. It was almost homely, after the attack of the piranha.

'I should have continued to reside in Chennai,' said Subbu dolefully. 'The living conditions were better than Mumbai and my family would have provided a sound social network.'

'Take me with you, Subbu,' said Tanya. She then raised a brow at me; a silent question about my opinion on the proceedings so far.

'What a strange man,' I said. 'Do you think it's all an act to scare us for some reason?'

'He looked pretty serious to me,' said Tanya. 'Do you think joining this place was a mistake, Mini?'

'I don't know about joining. But it was a mistake to not do

a credentials check on the CEO,' I replied.

'Well, things happened so quickly and we didn't know anyone here,' she said.

'Yes, with good reason. We don't normally hang out with people with suicidal tendencies,' I said.

'Maybe we can speak to Asha Lata. She might help us move out,' said Tanya, clearly clutching at straws. Asha Lata was the placement agent who had got us these jobs.

'Hmm, we'll see, shhh,' I hushed her as the door started to open again.

The fat girl from the corridor entered the room. She looked at Subbu, a stern look clouding her plump face.

'You! Are you in accounts? They are calling you there,' she instructed. Subbu hastily picked up his folder and rushed out. Then she turned to us.

'Right, so which one of you is Mini Shukla?' she asked. Tanya gratefully pointed at me as I nodded.

'You will report to me. Tanya Shrivastav, your team has not been decided yet. I am Shipra Gupta. Come with me, both of you.'

Shipra led me to an uninspiring cubicle and then gave me my password for the computer. She handed me some fat dossiers, containing within them what was bound to be terribly important information.

'You can go through these for the remaining part of the day,' she snapped at me. It was clear that she wasted no time on form, either literal or otherwise. In fact, when it came to the development of human elegance, Shipra was still with the apes.

'What about me?' asked Tanya, when my new boss started walking away.

'Oh, your cubicle is next to the restroom,' she declared with some relish. 'Go and sit there while they figure out what to do with you.'

Tanya went off to find her perch near the washrooms, obviously with some reluctance. I opened the dossier and started to read through the riveting information on the brand. True to promise, it turned out to be so enthralling that within fifteen minutes my eyelids started to feel heavy. Drooping, drooping, drooped.

'Chai?' asked someone, peering over one of the walls of the cubicle. I saw a boy of about twenty, grinning at me conspiratorially. I sat up straight, blinking furiously as he moved to the gap in the wall that served as the entrance to my seat. I saw that he was wearing a brown uniform that bore the legend 'Sawai Caterers' on the pocket. He was holding a tray of cups with hot tea swilling about. A more cheery sight could not have been arranged if Swiss Tourism had been at the job itself, adding just the right lake to the backdrop of a hundred perfectly symmetric majestic mountains and endless green lawns.

'Yes, please, thank you,' I said gratefully, hoping that he would not report my little nap to the power centre down the corridor.

He deposited a cup of tea on my desk.

'You are new to this place,' he observed.

I nodded as I picked up the tea. 'My first day,' I replied.

'*Hum hain* Shakti Prasad. *Kal se khaane ka* order *humein dene ka,'* he pronounced in Hindi that had been born north of the Vindhyas but had clearly been residing in Mumbai for some time now.

'Okay, Shakti Prasad,' I replied with a smile and took a sip. The tea was great, much better than what the machine used to dispense at the agency. Things were looking up already, as far as the caffeine addict in me was concerned.

'And be careful of that madam,' he winked in the direction of Shipra and then bounced off, balancing the teacups expertly as he went.

Well, this was encouraging. Not only were we blessed with a tyrannical super-boss, it was evident that the smaller life-forms were labelled highly avoidable too. At least the tea was eminently palatable, hot and sweet. I finished and decided to see how Tanya was faring. I found her new seat easily enough. Prakash was leaning over her cubicle wall, talking to her. He straightened when he saw me.

'Hi,' I said to Tanya, 'so this is your new cubicle. The stench led me here.'

'Har, har,' said Prakash, 'does that mean that the hygiene levels do not meet your lofty standards? I am destroyed.' He was smiling. I decided that I liked him.

'Well, let's just say that if I were the sanitary inspector around here, I would have eliminated some other roaches first,' I replied, looking in the direction of the CEO's office and displaying my sparkling wit. He grinned at me.

'I was just asking Tanya how your meeting with John Peters went. She was regaling me with all the names he called Avinash,' he said.

'I know! Did she tell you about how he nearly burst into tears at being compared to coffee machine leftovers? That was the funniest. Listen, Prakash, do you think we made a mistake about joining here?' I asked, lowering my voice.

'Yeah, tell us,' said Tanya. 'Else, I have Asha Lata's number on speed dial. She is our placement agent, the one who got us here.'

Prakash seemed to dwell on the question for a moment.

'Oh dear, that is a tough one to answer,' he finally said. 'I will think about it and let you know, alright? I have to get back to the dungeon now. See you later!'

After he'd left, Tanya told me that Prakash had been really friendly and had encouraged conversation.

'Well, at least not everyone in this place is a grade one ogre,' I said gratefully. 'Look, I better get back, I just came by to see where you were sitting. Are we doing drinks in the evening? Is Prithvi coming?'

'Sure. In fact, Subbu had come by some time back to use the washroom and I asked him to come along with us. He agreed quite happily.'

That was classic Tanya, friendly to a fault, one amongst her many. She had no discretion. I mean, we barely *knew* Subbu. However, the damage had been done and I had no time to argue with her.

'Well, if you think it's alright,' I said as I turned to go, 'let him come.'

I went back to my cubicle to find Shipra sitting on the corner of my desk. The desk looked weighed-in with worry about its immediate future. I looked at her, trying my best to be a picture of questioning innocence.

'Where were you?' she snapped when she saw me.

'I had gone to use the restroom,' I lied without thinking.

'Well, well, aren't you the smooth one,' she said, her eyebrows rising and a smirk spreading over the expanse of her face. 'Well, how about this? I know you were standing there chatting with that other girl!'

'Maybe I was, her cubicle is on the way. Is that a problem?' I asked, a little taken aback by her vehemence. It could be said that Shipra was all sunshine and sugary sweetness, but it would be a non-truth.

'That is most certainly a problem. You need to ask me if you want to take a break,' she said and stood, placing her hands on the desk to hoist herself up as she did so. The desk creaked under her weight.

'Are you serious? I need to ask you before I go to the loo?' I was genuinely incredulous. Surely she supported hygiene? Had respect for certain imminent and insistent bodily functions? Or was it time to break out the diapers?

'As we have just seen, we cannot trust you to actually use the washroom when you say so. So I am thinking, yes, you need to ask me when you take a break,' she said and stomped off. I saw my easy-going, chain-smoking ex-boss in the eye of my mind and cursed myself silently for having left the haven of his smoky aura. He would have neither noticed, nor minded, if I'd suddenly developed a weak bladder and took bathroom breaks every five minutes. Of course that was probably because he often took the aid of natural narcotics to get through the turmoil of life, but surely that was a minor issue. Suddenly I missed him intensely. Oh, to be able to breathe in the aroma of his Classic Milds again.

I sat down in my chair and stifled a groan. I stared at the dossiers unseeingly for the next two hours as I listened to U2 groan about bloody days of the week and dwelt on my recent decision to put an abrupt and gruesome end to my career by quitting a comfortable job to join this new place. At about seven in the evening, Shipra passed by my cubicle. She was carrying her bag. Using my strong powers of deduction, I immediately came to the conclusion that she was headed out. This meant that I needed to ask her something right then.

'Hey Shipra, do you think I can leave now? I can read the rest of this material tomorrow,' I called out. She stopped in her tracks, turned sharply on her figurative heels and came closer to where I was sitting.

'What is the annual turnover of our brand?' she asked.

I stared at her, completely blank. This was a question. It needed to be answered. The walls were closing in.

'I'm sorry?' I finally asked.

'Annual. Turnover. Brand,' she said. 'Tell me, which word is not clear?'

'Err, I know I read it somewhere,' I faltered even as I mentally delivered a slap across my forehead. 'I can check in a moment and let you know.'

She smirked. I stared at her, the shoulders wanting to slump in defeat.

'So you have spent the last several hours sitting here and still do not know the first thing about the brand. My guess is, you can leave. It is of no loss to anyone, least of all me,' she said and trotted off, smug in the knowledge that she had cut me down several sizes.

Feeling as proud as a bit of chewing-gum stuck under someone's shoes, I looked up the turnover and committed it to memory. Tanya stuck her head inside my cubicle.

'Why so morose?' she asked cheerfully. 'We can leave now. I saw your pet monster walking past, blood dripping from its fangs.'

I collected a glum handbag and a sad water bottle and we walked out. On our way to the pub, I told her what had happened with Shipra. She was most amused.

'It's not your fault, Mini,' she declared loyally, 'she has a need to establish herself as the superior in this equation. She will be fine once she knows you are good at your work. And hard-working. And efficient. And capable. Not to mention modest, humble and willing to let her take all the credit.'

I stared at her unseeingly. She caught my look.

'What? You will need to be all that if you want her to like you,' she said, as we entered the pub and walked to our regular table. 'Surely you realise that.'

My spirits dwindled a little more. I ordered some to replenish the stock.

Tanya dialled a number while I downed a large vodka with a dash of Sprite. I absently listened in to Tanya's side of the conversation.

'Hello, Asha Lata? It's me, Tanya.'

'Yes, we joined today.'

'Well, the first impression is not that great, you know.'

'No, no, the brand is great, I know that. It's just that the CEO was a little … abrasive.'

'I was thinking on the lines of quitting, actually.'

'Come on Asha Lata, surely those are strong swear words for a … situation … such as this?'

'What? How can that be?'

'I know that the job market is undergoing a bad patch but surely you can find us…'

'Hello?'

'Hello?'

Tanya hung up and shrugged at me. I was consuming my second drink of the evening and was now feeling fairly well-equipped to take on the world.

'No jobs, she says,' said Tanya and dug into a bowl of peanuts. Just then Prithvi, Tanya's long-time, long-suffering boyfriend made an appearance. He was a Software Something, a decidedly important designation.

'Wow, so you love the new office that much?' he said, pointedly looking at my empty and fast-getting-empty glasses. He bent down and kissed Tanya absently on her head of curls and slid in beside me.

'Shut up, Pri,' said Tanya affectionately. 'We have made the biggest, most colossal mistake of our short careers and the least you can do is run and get us refills.'

'And of course you are not rushing to conclusions, because after all, you have spent, let me see, a whole day there,' said Prithvi. I smacked his arm irritably.

'Hello Tanya. Hello Mini,' said someone from above our

heads. I thought I saw Subbu. Then I realised that it *was* Subbu. He was freshly showered and was wearing a shirt that could only be called 'striking' in polite society. If said society did not have to be polite, it would be called many other things. Tanya greeted him warmly by grunting in his general direction. Prithvi stood up and shook his hand. Subbu sat down. Prithvi ordered him a beer.

'You okay with that, man?' he asked as an afterthought.

'Yes, yes, I am perfectly alright with whatever you decide to order,' said Subbu. His beer arrived and he started taking small sips. I started to tell Prithvi about our disastrous day at work.

He whistled as I detailed out the finer nuances in Avinash's voice before he threw us out of his cabin and how Shipra was bent upon monitoring my every step, specially the ones that led to the toilet.

'It sounds like you'll are in a bit of a pickle,' he pronounced, when he got a chance to speak. 'It doesn't sound like his bosom is overflowing with love for the human race in general and three specimens in particular.' He turned to Subbu. 'What about you, Subbu? You haven't said much, what did you think?' he asked.

Subbu looked up. His pint of beer was almost over.

'I personally felt that the language that Mr Singh used was uncalled for,' he said primly. 'But I am willing to give him a second chance.'

Both Tanya and I guffawed at this. Subbu smiled uncertainly and downed the remainder of his beer as we started to talk of other things.

'Your beauty is very beauteous, Tanya,' he said, after a few minutes.

Tanya looked at him and then at me. Prithvi watched carefully.

'Thank you, Subbu. I think your brain is very brainy,' she said.

'And I think your luck is very lucky,' said Prithvi, 'that I know it's the beer talking. Ordering you a pint was not a very bright idea. Have you ever drunk anything before?'

'No, Mr Prithvi,' said Subbu happily, 'but my heart is filled with joy and solitude, I mean solidarity, for mankind.'

'Bullshit,' answered Prithvi. 'Get up, girls. We need to get this joker home.'

I was able to get Subbu's address from him and, on the cab-ride home, he sang us his favourite *raga*. We thanked him and deposited him home in Worli where he had taken digs at a hostel for working men. It was nearly one when we reached my home in Bandra that I shared with two other girls, Menaka and Urvashi. Tanya unkindly called them my *apsaras,* but if divine beauties were self-obsessed and incurably selfish, then Tanya had struck the nail on the head.

'Thanks for dropping me off, guys,' I said, as I started to let myself in. 'See you tomorrow, Tan.'

Tanya and Prithvi exchanged a look. I caught it and stopped in my tracks.

'What?' I barked gently at them.

'We wanted to tell you something, Mini. We were planning to do it tonight over drinks but then my dear wife-to-be invited that...' Prithvi started.

'Whoa! Stop right there! What did you just say? Did you just say "wife-to-be"? Did you? Did he?' I started jumping up and down with excitement.

'Yes!' the two shouted in unison.

I shrieked and continued to jump up and down.

'Oh my god! Oh my god! This is so great! I think I'm going to cry!' I threatened.

'You will do no such thing. You will now go inside and get some sleep and from tomorrow you shall start a diet that befits a maid of honour,' said Tanya.

They left and I found myself smiling and waving from the front door till they disappeared from view.

As I lay on my bed later that night, reliving the events of the day, I decided that the worst day of my career had ended on a good note after all.

# two

I reached office on time the next day, not wanting to upset the easily-riled Shipra. She was already seated at her desk and looked like she had been there for some time. A bowl of milk lay on her desk with some abandoned wheat-flakes floating in it like capsized boats. Milk and cornflakes could not have made her the size she was, I thought charitably to myself as I approached her.

'Hey, Shipra,' I said gingerly. 'How are you doing?'

She looked up but did not say a word. What was this, the attack of the beady-eyed? A *maun-vrat*? I continued to smile apprehensively, she continued to stare at me, the earth continued to turn on its axis. Then, mercifully, the phone rang.

'Hello? Yes, Mr Singh? Yes, I am prepared. I am coming right over. Hmm? Alright, I will get them along.'

She replaced the receiver and heaved herself up.

'Mr Singh wants to see us. Call your friend also. On the phone. No need to go there,' she said, and started to collect her files. I groaned inwardly and went to my cubicle. I tried Tanya's extension. As expected, there was no reply. I stood on my toes to take a furtive look in Shipra's direction over the wall of my cubicle. She seemed to be busy. I dialled Tanya's mobile phone number. She answered on the fifth ring.

'Tanya! Where are you? Avinash Singh wants to meet us. Now!'

'What? Oh, dash it! I overslept. I will start in two minutes.'

'My god! Are you still in bed?'

'Well, not anymore. See you.'

She hung up. I was saddened to realise that this was possibly the last time I had spoken to Tanya as a colleague. Avinash would waste no time in firing her when he found out that she was late on her second day at work. Of course, that was not a bad thing.

'If you have finished day-dreaming, maybe we can leave?'

I jumped up. 'Of course, Shipra. I … err … Tanya will join us shortly,' I said and picked up a notebook and a pencil from the desk. 'Let's go.'

Shipra shrugged and trundled in the direction of the CEO's cabin. I followed her meekly, marvelling at the girth of her sizeable bottom. We passed a couple of people and both of them threw ingratiating hellos at Shipra. I was surprised. From what I had seen of her gentle demeanour and pleasing manner, I would have thought that people would throw up their heads in extended howls and proceed to swiftly run in the opposite direction.

Shipra ignored the pretty secretary who was sitting in her usual spot, instead going straight up to Avinash's cabin and knocking on the door. Avinash was standing at the window with some tissue in his hand. Prakash was at his side. Avinash swiped the tissue across the ledge and peered at the faint line of dust that appeared on it.

'Look at this!' he bellowed at Prakash. 'Am I paying them to clean my office? Am I? Am I, I ask!'

'Yes, sir,' said Prakash calmly.

'Then either get them to clean this up so it doesn't look like a garbage dump or that is where their bodies will land,' he screamed.

I gasped involuntarily at this definitely mafiaesque statement. Avinash turned to us.

'Hmm, Shipra, are the reports ready?' he asked. 'Let us take a look.'

Shipra smiled and handed some papers over.

'I have also emailed them, Avinash,' said Shipra.

'I know, I know. I've been busy. I couldn't look through them,' he said grumpily. I tried to blend into the flowery print on the chair.

'Okay, so this looks alright. This store needs to pick up. This continues to do well. The sales incentive seems to have worked...' He continued to comment on things that I had no idea about. Shipra nodded and took down notes. He seemed to be almost fond of her, I realised with a shock. Finally he put the papers down.

'Well, this is good,' he said, as Prakash put down some milk and cookies on the table. Avinash picked up one cookie, dipped it into his glass of milk, and started chomping. My stomach growled, protesting a missed breakfast. I hoped nobody had heard it and that Avinash would offer us a cookie before too long. He did not.

'Let us talk about the promotion we plan to do with *Azura* now,' he said, taking another cookie from the plate. They were chocolate chip, I noticed, as I furtively wiped the little bit of drool that had come out of the corner of my mouth.

'Yes, sir. I have spoken to *Azura* and they are willing to put our brand on the front cover of the magazine. But they insist that we get a model and pay for her,' Shipra said.

'I know just the girl,' he said unexpectedly. 'You need to get in touch with Anuradha Menon. What a figure! How fresh! Such long limbs! Such lovely, dusky skin. Indian mother, Irish father, best of both worlds. Ah ha!' Avinash seemed lost in his reverie for a moment.

'Where is that other girl?' he suddenly barked at me. I floundered under the unexpected attack.

'She! Will! Be! In! Any! Minute! Now!' I said, hoping that I had covered my nervousness with my excitement.

Prakash smiled and spoke for the first time. 'She had not swiped her card when I checked five minutes ago. Maybe running a little late? Perhaps a little, um, hungover?' he said smoothly. I found myself staring at him with an open mouth. How did he know we had gone out drinking the previous night? Had he also been at the pub? Why hadn't he come and said hello then?

'Listen to me, what is your name,' said Avinash. I tore my eyes away from Prakash in a hurry. 'You will take care of the *Azura* initiative. Shipra, brief her about what we are trying to achieve here. She comes from an environment of overwhelming mediocrity and may find it difficult to adjust to one of excellence. John Peters may have screwed up but we need to live with his mistakes.'

Well, how flattering. I had never been called a mistake before in my life.

'Alright, sir, should I introduce her to Clients Are Us?' Shipra asked. I knew Clients Are Us was the advertising agency that handled the JRE business. I puffed up with self-importance at the thought of being the client instead of the slave for the first time. This would be great. I would command them at all hours of the day and night. I would call them at unreasonable hours and make unreasonable requests. I would ruin their social lives and their weekends. Finally I would have my revenge and I would have it cold.

'No! She doesn't need any agency support. They are billing us too much as it is. Let her handle it on her own,' said Avinash. The sound of a broken heart resounded through the hallways of JR Enterprises.

At this point, Tanya burst into the room.

'I am so sorry, sir,' she said. 'My key wouldn't work and I could not just leave the house open so I had to hunt for a locksmith.' I was widening and narrowing my eyes at Tanya in an attempt to warn her but she would not look at me. After going on for some time about the difficulty of finding locksmiths at early hours of the morning, she finally tapered off under Avinash's stern gaze and looked at him hopelessly.

'Get out,' said Avinash. 'If you don't want to work, there is no need for you to come in and use up the oxygen.' Tanya stood there, frozen to the spot. Prakash melted away but was back in the office within a minute.

'Why are you still here?' Avinash shouted, when Tanya seemed unable to move. 'Haven't I expressed myself clearly? I know what drivel that John Peters has told you and the only thing you need to know is — every word he said is true. I am a monster and I will eat you alive if you don't do exactly as I say. Lying, lazy, incompetent piece of—'

Tanya seemed to believe his every word and turned hastily to leave. I stared at the last bit of cookie lying on the plate morosely, wishing that the chips hid traces of arsenic. Not too much of course, just enough to ensure a long, painful death for the man.

'And don't think that I don't know what you are up to. I have my people everywhere,' he continued to shout. 'Go and ask Asha Lata or Anuradha Paudwal or whoever the hell you like. And you haven't made a mistake by joining, I have made a mistake by not firing you yet.' Tanya scurried out like a scared mouse. I suppressed my natural urge to take the now-empty plate of cookies and smash it on his head. Repeatedly. Prakash was still smiling.

'You! Get started on *Azura*. Shipra, good work again. Out, both of you,' Avinash stomped off. Shipra simpered and collected her things. Well, at least she was good at her work. I could ignore her obnoxious nature and focus on learning the ropes from her. I followed her out of the cabin.

'Mini!' the pretty secretary called out to me as we started to pass by. 'Could you just sign some papers? HR has left them for you.' Shipra shrugged at me and walked on. I took the papers from the girl and started to sign them before realising that they had nothing to do with HR at all.

'Don't trust Prakash,' the girl whispered, still looking studiously at the papers. 'He is the mole.'

Such intrigue. I smiled at the girl. She did not smile back. I looked at the expansive Shipra as she turned the corner and was no more in sight. I considered it safe to talk.

'How do you mean "mole"?' I asked as I folded the papers and put them away.

'Well, he is Avinash's spy, you know. Anything and everything that is said around the office is filtered back to Avinash. There is nothing like a non-infiltrated grapevine.'

'Really? I didn't know but thanks, I will watch out from now on,' I said as I caught sight of a book lying face down on her table; *Mysteries of World War Two Solved*, it promised.

'I'm Mumtaaz,' she said.

'Good to meet you. Listen, I'd love to stay and chat but I better go and see how Tanya is doing,' I said.

'Oh, yes, yes, go, but Tanya is not sitting by the restroom anymore,' said Mumtaaz.

'Really? That's great! Where is she now?' I asked happily.

'By the lost and found closet,' said Mumtaaz expressionlessly.

'Uh oh' came to mind.

'Would you know where that is?' I asked.

'It's by the cafeteria kitchen,' said Mumtaaz sadly. 'In the besement — it will take you ten minutes just to walk down there.'

Well, I did not have ten minutes. I was also starving. I

decided to see Tanya later in the day and hurried back to my desk. I found the cafeteria extension on the list of phone numbers pinned to the cubicle wall and dialled it. Shakti Prasad announced his name grandly at the other end. I asked him if he could get me something to eat. He promised me a plate of poha. Having taken care of the truly critical matters, I decided to remind Shipra about the *Azura* briefing. I approached her desk and found her positively glowing while she chatted to a man with his back to me. He turned around as I reached Shipra's desk and I did a little glowing of my own. The boy was positively delicious looking. I did a quick assessment. Lanky, nice complexion and good shoes — just the way I liked them. He smiled at me. I offered a smile and hastily withdrew it as Shipra scowled at me.

'What do you want?' she said, eyebrows still knitted.

'Shipraaaaa, come on, at least introduce the new girl to me,' the boy said in a lazy drawl.

'Hey, I'm Mini,' I extended a hand, wishing — not for the first time — that my name had a nice, romantic touch to it, instead of ending before it began. His hand was warm and dry. Brownie points. His name was Varun, he said. I wanted to ask him if his last name was a phone number but decided that such cheesiness would probably be better left for when the boss was not staring at one like one was a specimen of a particularly disgusting species of vermin.

'Shipra,' I turned to her. 'I just wanted to check when you would be free to brief me about *Azura*.'

'What do you want to know?' said Shipra evenly.

This was strange. I had no idea where to start.

'I have no idea where to start,' I said.

'Listen, I think you guys are busy. Ships, I will drop by later. Have fun, Mini,' said Varun and took his sunny presence out of Shipra's cubicle. It became dank again. I found myself staring at a frosty-eyed Shipra.

'Err, alright, so maybe I should prepare a list of questions and maybe you can answer them?' I offered.

'Maybe,' she said and turned to her computer. What was this? Were she and I, unbeknownst to me, lovers? Were we currently in the middle of a spat? Was I supposed to get her flowers and chocolates? Ready to scream, I left her cubicle and went to my desk, where Shakti Prasad was just putting my plate of poha down. I had a sudden urge to burst out crying.

'Chai?' he asked, completely oblivious to the emotional meltdown threatening to take place in front of him.

I nodded. He turned to go and saw my face, perhaps the size of a single Froot Loop at that moment, and stopped in his tracks. He cleared his throat a couple of times. 'Arrey, madam. Don't mind what she says. She is like that only. It's not your fault,' he said.

At this unconditional support, I cheered up somewhat and started shovelling the poha inside my mouth. I asked him if he knew where Tanya was sitting now. He did, and shared her new extension number before taking his happy, food-bearing presence elsewhere. After the food had raised my spirits, I dialled it.

'Hey, I believe I have lost a Tanya. Slightly dangerous, largely harmless. Have you found her,' I quipped.

'Shut up,' I got for my efforts. She was obviously furious.

'This is corporate no-man's land, Mini,' she said. 'I have only heard the clanging of pots and pans all morning. And the way they did it! I rushed out of Avinash's office to my desk, except that there was no desk. Gone! And someone came and told me that it had reappeared here. It took me half an hour just to find it.'

'Oh, so that's what Prakash had gone out for,' I groaned, mentally delivering a tight slap to myself for taking him for a genial bloke.

'Have they assigned you to a team yet?' I asked, though I knew the answer already.

'No! I don't think they plan to either. I am just supposed to rot here. Just because I was late. Once. At the agency, I never got to office before eleven,' she whined.

'Maybe you should spend your free time planning for the wedding,' I joked. 'When do you plan to do it by the way?'

'October. Well, get back to work then. I will see you at lunch.'

I hung up and figured I had better get down to some real work. I opened a Word document and began to type out a list of questions for Shipra.

1. How did you get so fat?

2. Are you and Varun an item?

3. If yes, how do I snatch him from you?

4. What would be your preferred mode of death at my hands — stabbing, poisoning or lynching?

I sighed and deleted the list. If I mailed it to her by accident, that would be the end of the world as I knew it. I worked for the next couple of hours, thinking hard about all the information I would need about the *Azura* initiative. All I knew about *Azura* was that it was a fashion magazine. What exactly we were planning to do with them was anyone's guess. After running a quick check for spelling and grammatical errors, I emailed the document to Shipra. I looked at the time and realised that it was almost lunch hour. I called Tanya again and asked her if she would meet me at the cafeteria.

'I'll be there,' she replied dolefully. I grabbed my bag and skipped to the lift, which, when it reached my floor, opened to reveal an occupant.

Oh joy!

Varun, in all his handsome glory. He smiled as I jumped in.

'How's it going?' he opened the conversation as he pressed six on the elevator panel.

'Oh, I'm hard at work,' I said, hoping to impress on him my industrious attitude.

'Ah good ... I believe things are not going very well with the big man? Ships told me,' he said, not giving away too much.

'Sort of,' I said noncommittally. At the sixth floor, we got out and walked towards the tables that were buzzing with people filling their trays with food and chatting and eating. Tanya was standing by the soft drink vending machine. She saw me with Varun and her eyes widened. She nearly jogged all the way to us.

'I'm Tanya, Mini's friend. I sit by the lost and found closet,' she said, holding out her hand.

'Charmed, I'm sure,' laughed Varun as he took it.

'Are you going to have lunch with us?' I asked him invitingly.

'Sure, come on. I can't see Ships anywhere anyway,' he said and started handing out trays to us.

I coyly served myself some salad. Tanya saw me and opened her mouth, to verbalise, I'm sure, her concern about this unnatural behaviour. I glowered at her and she shut up.

Varun was a fashion designer with the company, he told us when we were all seated. Shipra and he had gone to the same college. 'She was always a *muggu*,' he said. 'Always kept her nose buried in books.'

'You seem quite close,' I said, hoping to fish out some information, but Varun only nodded and did not say anything.

'So tell me, what do you girls do after work?'

'At the agency, we used to go out pubbing and bowling, watch movies or just hang out with people from work or Prithvi, my boyfriend … fiancé,' Tanya said. 'Now, I'm not sure what we will end up doing.'

'Well, we can go out if you like,' said Varun. I did some mental cartwheels at this.

'Sure thing. Give your number to Mini and we will plan something,' Tanya closed the deal perfectly.

'May I join you?' I looked up and saw Mumtaaz, holding her tray of food. I welcomed her and started to introduce Tanya, but she interrupted, saying she knew her already.

'My job requires me to keep a check on everyone,' she said. Tanya laughed and then realised that Mumtaaz was not joking.

'How is it going with the bat from hell?' Varun asked Mumtaaz.

'Same old. I get blasted about everything. Since morning I have been called a useless piece of junk, something even the most indiscriminating cat would not drag in and oh, also, an overall insult to humanity,' she said, violently digging her fork into the rice.

Varun whistled.

'Well, I'm glad we're not the only ones to get tossed about like clothes in a washing machine on rage mode,' said Tanya. 'What I don't get is why people stick on in this company.'

'They don't really,' explained Varun. 'Attrition is at an all-time high. Even the Mittals are asking questions now, I've heard. But they do stick around for a reasonable amount of time for various reasons — the company pays better than the industry average. The brand is doing very well and it looks good on your *résumé* to have been part of a shining, successful team. Plus, other jobs are difficult to find in this climate.'

'And some of us are just suckers for punishment,' said Mumtaaz.

Just then, Avinash walked into the cafeteria and served himself some food. He ate regular food. I would have imagined a steady diet of humans limbs with fresh blood sauce would have been the only thing to hit the spot for him.

'I notice the monster eats with us,' I said softly.

'Yes,' said Varun. 'He sits at the same empty table every day. Anyone who wants can go and sit with him and discuss anything they like. New ideas, innovations, plans — he offers to listen to anyone about everything. No one ever goes, of course. They fear for their lives.'

'And more importantly, appetites, I am sure,' said Tanya.

'Whatever happened to those father figure bosses that I heard about at my secretarial course,' grumbled Mumtaaz as she got up. 'I need to run back — I have to book some stuff for him. Keep your ears to the ground, comrades.'

After lunch, Varun and I decided to drop Tanya off at her cubicle. The end of the earth, she called it. It was a truly miserable spot and actually shared its back wall with the cafeteria kitchen. It seemed to be JRE's equivalent of the naughty child's corner, the Alcatraz where people who displeased Avinash were moved before being asked to leave altogether. Wisely, I kept my impressions unverbalised. Leaving Tanya with her computer and phone for company, we trundled back up to our floor. Varun did not say much and I feared that I had spoiled everything by speaking too much. Or too little. Or saying something very funny. Or pissing him off because he did not get it. Waving casually to me, he sauntered off in the direction of the design studio where all the creative juices flowed together in one comprehensive stream. I went back to my decidedly less glamorous place and checked my mail. There was no reply from Shipra. Well, there was no work till there was work. I leant back into my seat and decided to dream a little about the lovely lunch and lovelier lunch partner.

'If you are done relaxing, maybe you can be of some use around here, though I am fairly certain it is technically impossible given your sub-human intelligence,' said Shipra. I jumped to attention at this sudden but expected attack.

'Sure, what is it?'

'Take these to the agency. Tell them these are the approved briefs and try not to take too long,' she said and gave me a package.

'Clients Are Us? Who do I need to meet? Do they know I'm coming?' I asked after her.

'Maybe you should have used your morning finding out these details instead of practising the art of coquetry,' she said insultingly and walked away.

Humph. Well, this was really too much. I should probably go right in and tell her that, as my boss, she was responsible for my development as a professional and that she had to stop being childish and insecure and get a grip. Oh, and lose a couple of tyres.

I decided that begging Mumtaaz for help was a wiser option.

Mumtaaz was at her desk, fortunately, and able to give me the agency's address and the names of the executives who handled the JRE account. I went from Lower Parel to Nariman Point to deliver the parcel and stopped only for a vada-pav on my way back. Still, being Mumbai, it took me a couple of hours. When I got back, I saw Prakash walking away from Shipra's cubicle. I went over to her desk and noticed a couple of cups lying empty on her desk. He had clearly spent some quality time with her.

'I've handed over the parcel,' I told Shipra. She gave me a look that rendered air-conditioning redundant.

'Wonderful. Fantastic. Great job,' she said, in a feeble attempt at sarcasm. She looked through a pile of books lying next to her and picked out one to slide in my direction. 'Some of it is highlighted in yellow. Type it all in a Word document.'

I picked up the book. 'What is it for?' I asked.

'Excuse me?' she said, unable to believe that Oliver Twist had asked for some more.

'What am I doing this for?' I repeated. 'I mean, towards what purpose am I making this document?'

'Towards the purpose of keeping you out of my sight,' she said. 'And oh, research, if you like. Now get started.'

'Right.' I decided to stick to my guns and display some valour in the face of fire. 'What about the *Azura* project though? I needed you to give me—' at this point, her look became positively frosty, '—uh, right, so I will start on this document,' I finished weakly and walked back to my desk. Well, no one had said corporate life would be easy. This was A Challenge. A Challenge that needed to be Dealt With. I got back to my seat and tried to think of ways to Deal With The Challenge. Nothing came to mind so I started to type out the many, many parts that had been highlighted in the book.

Towards the last part of the day, I received a reply to my questions from Boss Lady.

1. Who is our key contact at *Azura*?
   Please don't waste my time asking such mundane things. Surely you can figure this out on your own.

2. What is the objective of the *Azura* initiative?
   Cover page.
3. What are the terms and conditions of our agreement
   with *Azura*?
   Ask key contact.

And the rest of the questions were answered in a similar vein. I sighed and shut my mailbox. At least something was established here. She was deliberately trying to shut me out. These were perfectly legitimate questions, and she needed to answer them to brief me. If she did not want to part with any information, I figured it was back to first principles again. I got Mumtaaz to give me the number of *Azura* magazine and decided to get in touch with them immediately. 'Hello,' said a remarkably bored voice at the *Azura* office.

'Madam, good evening,' I said in my politest voice. 'I need to speak to someone in the editorial department.'

'Connecting,' she snapped and the phone started ringing again.

'Yes?' A hassled-sounding voice answered.

'Hello, I am calling from JR Enterprises. I need to speak to the person we have been in touch with regarding the cover page,' I said, hoping to break the ice.

'Yes, but who is it that you want?' the voice asked.

'Err, I don't know. Uh, my boss is sick and I am looking after this now and I cannot get in touch with her to get the relevant person's name…' I was clutching at straws.

'Oh I see. Well, call back in a bit and I'll ask the editor in the meanwhile. My name is Jaya,' she said and disconnected the phone. Not bad at all, I thought. I could do this without Shipra.

The phone rang again. It was Tanya.

'I have been sitting here all day. I tried to call HR but they say that the staff's job descriptions were handled by John Peters and he has quit. Do you think they'll pay my salary or will I just be considered a potted plant? A plant that does not even need sunlight and fresh air, judging by this place?'

'I don't know, but believe me, it's not that great here either,' I consoled her.

'Oh, and I just spoke to Subbu. He called to apologise most humbly for last night. Now, listen to this. Apparently Prakash went to talk to him this morning and Subbu ended up telling him about our little outing. That is how Avinash knew that we had gone out drinking. I'm telling you, our phones may well be bugged,' said Tanya.

'Stop sounding like Mumtaaz,' I said irritably. 'I need to go now. You find something to do.'

'Do what?' she wailed. 'I have already called Pri thrice today. He has work. You have work. Subbu has work. Only I don't have anything to do!'

'Count your blessings,' I said and disconnected the call.

Shipra came bustling into my cubicle. I noticed a trail of smoke billowing about in the region of her ears.

'How dare you lie about me to *Azura*?' she yelled.

'I'm sorry?'

'Stop looking so innocent. Did you or didn't you tell Jaya that I was sick?'

'Oh that. Yes I did. I needed to lie because I had no other way of finding out who we were talking to in the magazine,' I tried to explain.

'Well, listen to me clearly. I don't care how much or to whom you lie. Just don't ever mention my name again, you hear?'

'Yes, of course,' I whimpered.

She stormed back to her cubicle. Weren't we in a happy place now, I thought grumpily to myself. She would not share any details about the project and she was making it really difficult for me to find out on my own.

Only one thing was certain, I had to figure out a sustainable strategy to last in this maddening place.

# three

The next couple of months passed me by in a flurry of supremely critical work such as fetching and delivering parcels, photocopying and filing thousands of documents and typing out paragraphs from books when they could have easily been electronically scanned.

I felt that I had gone back a couple of years to the time I was fresh out of business school and resultantly at the bottom of the food chain. Only this was worse. At that time, I really was of no better use than performing the most basic of tasks, but now, now I could do more than this. Hell, Avinash had given me the all-important *Azura* project to take care of. In the time I had left after accomplishing the hundreds of useless tasks that Shipra set out for me every day, I tried to take baby-steps towards making that project a success and thereby preserve my job. Despite my best efforts, thus far I had only succeeded in discovering the person who was dealing with JR Enterprises at the magazine's end. This I had achieved by taking the initiative of delving into Shipra's desk when she was not around. Being technologically savvy, I had first tried to break into her mailbox, but she had protected it with a series of passwords. Fortunately though, she did have some mailers signed by this person on her desk and I committed the name to the deepest recesses of my memory. After this criminal act, I worried a bit about getting caught and being sent to jail, and therefore had to spend some time rehearsing the passionate speech that I would deliver in the courthouse.

*Yeh jhooth hai,* Judge *sahab, mere saath na-insaafi hui hai.*

When I did not get caught however, like all natural-born criminals, I fervently thanked The Person in Charge of the Universe and carried on with my work.

To my pleasant surprise, rare as they had become these days, the woman I was dealing with at the magazine was a non-monstrous, perfectly normal girl called Zoya. She told me everything about the workings of the fashion magazine and our deal with them after I fell at her feet and declared my ignorance of what I needed to do, and also deposited a bundle of Ferraro Rocher chocolates in her lap.

'Some magazines have started selling their cover page to advertisers,' she had explained. 'Essentially what happens is that you decide on the model and the clothes she will wear for the cover of that issue. The logo of your brand is prominently displayed on the clothes, of course. We carry the interview of the cover-girl in our issue. The interview deals with all sorts of things that our readers are dying to know about her, like her nail-painting routine for example, but you can get your model to also talk about your brand. Of course, the corporate and the magazine need to agree on the model because she affects both our brands.'

I dwelt on the absence of ethics in the system. Readers paid for magazines not realising that their favourite models and actors were trained by corporate houses to articulate the benefits of their brands. Maybe it was time for an evangelist who could cure the system of all ills? Someone smart and conscientious and who would look good in a superhero costume? Namely, me? Taking the corrupt out of corruption. Leaving behind only squeaky-clean deals. And the 'ion', of course.

'What happened?' asked Zoya after a couple of moments, as I sat lost in my do-gooder's reverie. I shook myself and returned to reality. This was the world of Avinash Singh. Sir, sir, yes, sir, I was a minion who followed orders, sir.

'What do you think of Anuradha Menon, Zoya? Will she fit the bill?' I asked.

'I think so, though I will need to get her approved by the editor,' replied Zoya after thinking for a moment. 'But yes, she is a bright young model, doing very well on the ramp and planning a foray into Bollywood. She should do.'

'Great! Thank you so much, I hope you enjoy your chocolates,' I said and rose to leave.

'I believe what you need to say these days is that you hope they don't go to my hips and thighs,' said Zoya, a worried frown breaking her grin as she peeled the wrapper off one. 'Because though this month's edition carries "Seventeen Startling Ways to Break the Blubber Bubble Forever", I doubt if even one of them works.'

I was very chuffed at this breakthrough. At last I knew what was expected of me when people flung phrases like

'The *Azura* Initiative' (and sometimes, just 'The Project', unfailingly tempting me to ask 'Blair Witch?') at me. They were referring to *this* borderline illegal activity. Ah well, everyone needs to get their hands dirty, I declared to myself, and if I needed to wade through this sewage to climb to the top of the ladder that led to corporate heaven, I would be the dirtiest pig that ever waddled to where the swill was. Oink.

I now needed to get in touch with the new hope of the modelling world. This would require activities that are contained in the phrase searching high and searching low. In other words, I leaned back in my chair and typed 'Anuradha Menon' in my search engine. The holy world of the internet threw back millions and millions of answers my way. Only the pure could pick out the one true answer and I was it I decided, as I found a clean-looking website that did not want me to download screensavers featuring lush waterfalls or busty women or busty women under lush waterfalls.

Anuradha Menon was a lovely woman, I realised with a sharp pang of jealousy as I went through her pictures on the website. Very tall, somewhat angular, dusky and with lustrous hair. It was hardly a surprise that she was doing so well at her job. Unlike some of us, I grumbled inwardly.

'And who are you making faces at?' I heard Varun's voice. He was smiling and looking at me over my cubicle wall. I immediately wished I had worn my new green silk top to work instead of the ratty kurti that I had finally pulled on.

'Oh hey, stranger,' I said with as much nonchalance as I could muster under the thumping call of the hormonal heart. 'We haven't seen you in these parts for a while now.'

'I was travelling on work, didn't you know? We covered the entire north zone in about a week: Delhi, Chandigarh, Patiala, Jalandhar, the works. I ate more butter than paranthas, oye hoy, *mar jaawan gur khaake,*' he sighed. 'But to go back to where we were, who were you making faces at?'

'Oh that,' I said, slightly embarrassed. 'Nothing much. Anuradha Menon, shining star of the modelling world and heiress to the Bollywood fortune. Coming soon to theatres near you.'

'Do you like Bollywood?' he asked.

'Who doesn't?' I said, and immediately wondered if that had been the correct answer. Maybe he was above Bollywood, floating in the stratosphere far, far above, containing offbeat Hungarian films followed by discussions on camera angles and light. Maybe 'the dramatic visual imagery not-so-subtly confesses to us the rich dramatic interplay of culture and music' would have been a better response?

'That's true. Everyone does. In fact, we are working on a special Bollywood range for the next collection, you know. It's such fun,' he said to my relief, and then added unexpectedly, 'In fact, I have been watching a lot of films because of work. Would you like to come along one of these days?'

'Absolutely,' I said, while inside my heart burst into song — in this case an appropriate *Aapki nazron ne samajha pyaar ke kaabil mujhe.*

'Well, see you around then. I'll go meet Ships now,' he said and walked off.

This was a good turn to the day, I thought. Now back to Anuradha Menon and her whereabouts.

The phone rang. It was Tanya.

'The florist is here with the catalogues,' she said. 'Do you think you can come over and offer opinions?' I put my head in the hand that was not holding the receiver.

'Tell me you're kidding,' I pleaded. Tanya had had enough of waiting and had decided that the project she would be working on would be her perfect wedding day. Recently she had taken to asking suppliers over to office for extended discussions.

'I won't because I'm not. I like the orchids but I know that you might have a point of view. Is Lardie around?' she asked.

I took a peek at Shipra's desk. Varun was sitting with her and they had some designs spread out in front of them that they seemed to be discussing.

'She is but I think I can spare a few minutes,' I said and stole out quietly. If Shipra saw me sneaking out, she was bound to give me some more photocopying to do. She didn't and I sprinted all the way to Tanya's corner of slime. Experience had taught me that waiting for the lifts when proceeding to head in the general direction of those wastelands wasted time.

Tanya was sitting with a nervous-looking character, a bony man with a thin moustache who got up as I came in.

'Hello, Mini, this is Samrat Singh of Samrat Phoolwalla,' she introduced us without looking up from an album that contained pictures of floral decorations that Samrat Phoolwalla had done for numerous weddings and functions. For a moment I felt that I had slipped into an alternate universe.

'The white ones look good, Tan,' I offered, shaking off the surreal feeling and peering at the pictures. 'Maybe for the reception? In glass jars. Long, green stems, huh?'

'Hmm, I was thinking purple orchids in blue Khurja pottery,' Tanya said and then turned to Samrat Singh. 'Samrat ji, I need to spend more time on this. Leave this album and your rate card here. I will get in touch with you in a week or so.'

Samrat Singh nodded furiously and after a nod in my direction, beat a retreat.

'Varun asked me out for a movie,' I broke my news as Tanya filed away Samrat Singh's visiting card.

'Oh? When? Pri is travelling the whole of next week,' said Tanya.

'Not the extended family, Tan, just me,' I pointed to myself.

'Ooh! Like a *date* date,' she concluded excitedly.

'Well, if repetition signifies just the two of us, then yes,' I replied and got up. 'I have to run now. Lardie may be done any minute. Are you serious about this, Tanya? This wedding preparation business?'

'What else do I do while I wait for them to fire me, Mini? This is like when I was young and did something that made Mom mad. Instead of giving me a couple of sound slaps and getting it out of her system, she wouldn't speak to me at all for a day or two. It was so torturous to just wait for the punishment.'

'My mom never waited. She swiftly delivered it, on both cheeks,' I said, fondly reminiscing. 'Anyway, later.'

I ran all the way back. Shipra was still at her desk with Varun. I was safe. For now. I started to crunch some numbers that she had asked me to analyse. I only got tasks these days, with no objective, no method and sometimes even no reason. Sometimes I wallowed in the murky waters of self-pity. Most of the time, there was no time for even that.

In the last couple of months, I had gathered some information about Shipra from various sources, most of them part of the Sutta Club that met outside the building, near the achingly romantic garbage dump. The stress of working with Shipra had been all the excuse I had needed to get back to the stick. Smokers were treated like lepers in JR Enterprises, much like everywhere else in the city, and were required to step so far outside the office complex that they often needed to ask for directions back.

The Sutta Club had a generous sprinkling of designers, most of them insanely fashionable. I had never seen Varun there, though. Some nerdy bespectacled managers, fast developing paunches over skinny legs, hung about too, as did an occasional brand management servant-girl like myself. The atmosphere was one of congeniality, and I often heard snippets that were of immense importance to an information-deprived soul like mine. Tanya refused to come out with me, claiming that the second-hand smoke gave her a headache in the knee, a joke she'd found funny since kindergarten. Mumtaaz gamely accompanied me though. I thought it made her feel more like a spy than ever before.

'**If** only people knew that I'm not really a smoker,' she told me smugly after a couple of days, holding a lit cigarette in her fingers.

'They do, Mumtaaz. Any smoker can tell from a mile away that you haven't taken a single drag in your life,' I said, and immediately regretted it as her face fell. 'But you're getting better everyday, really. Why don't you go and chat up Mukesh from IT now?'

Mumtaaz ambled off to tempt state secrets out of Mukesh from IT who, unable to handle so much attention, nearly singed himself with his cigarette as he gawped at the attractive Matahari in front of him.

Through the Sutta Club, I found out that Shipra was a star performer in the office. She was completely committed to her work and equally insecure about her place in office. She had no friends at work and Varun was the only one she spoke to. She had had a series of assistant managers reporting to her and each had left citing her as the sole reason for bringing them to the brink of insanity. Wagers had already been placed as to how long I would last, and it was unflattering to learn that no one was setting too much store by me. Shipra was also a power centre in the company, the best-performing marketing manager for the brand and one of Avinash's hot favourites, I learnt.

Avinash himself was understood to have quite the roving eye. The girls at work had nothing to fear, however. Apparently he only played in the top league. An equally powerful ex-wife, supposedly lurking around somewhere in the background, had reportedly given it as good as she got while they were still married. They now spoke to each other only for the sake of the children, who, one hoped, were inheriting nothing from either parent. The fights had been legendary and the arguments ceaseless. He now lived alone in a beautiful house in Colaba. The house was perfectly done, the privileged few who had been inside said; all giant heads of Thai Buddhas and fountains and gorgeous chandeliers, if one liked that sort of thing.

From behind the smokescreen set up in those short and casual chats, things finally began to assume a degree of clarity for me. And to think people said nothing good would ever come out of smoking.

Varun called me later that evening and asked me if I was willing to watch a late show. I silently whooped and agreed to meet him at Inox theatre late in the evening. Who needed sleep? No one. Sleep was overrated. I was young and needed to be restless.

I went home and saw that my *apsaras*, Urvashi and Menaka, were still at work. The tap in the bathroom was dripping and Urvashi had reneged on her promise to call the plumber yet again. After a few deep breaths to remain all Zen, I decided to cook some dinner. After checking the refrigerator for supplies, I promptly dialled my mother for her aloo-tamatar recipe. Again. You really should write it down, my mother told me. I agreed with her cheerfully and scribbled it on a scrap of paper that would be lost before the pressure-cooker whistled for the second time. My mother meandered about for a while and then jumped to the only topic that she was interested in these days. My marriage to a suitable boy, she said, was not something that would just happen. One needed to make efforts. I should tell her if there is anyone, she comfortingly rubbed it in. There isn't, I pricked her bubble of hope. Arranged marriage, she hesitatingly suggested. Over my dead body, I declared. Accepting the arranged option was to give up on love, on the perfect man and on life, I declared. The niceties done, she told me about the troubles the old car and the old dog were having. I felt terribly homesick. Dad took the phone from her.

'When are you coming home?' Always the ice-breaker, ever since I had moved away from home.

'Soon, Pa, soon,' I said, unable to see myself walking up to Lardie to ask for leave.

'How's work?'

'It's okay.'

'How's work?' he asked again. I grinned to myself. The old fox had not lost his touch.

'It's a little different from what I expected. A little more — challenging.'

'I see. How's Tanya doing?'

'Her problem is just the opposite, not enough challenge. Or work, for that matter.'

'Hmmm, how long will you give it?'

'I've just started. I have a project now. I need to crack it before things can improve. Don't worry, it's going to be fine.'

'Of course it will, *you* are handling it,' said the doting padre. That was the thing about blind parental love, it kept you buoyant in the aforementioned sewer. Parents of junior managers probably imagined their offspring to be superstars in the making, their over-achieving, nerdy children who did remarkably well at school and made it to the best business-schools, only to land in places like JR Enterprises and be shown what the smallest-fish way of life was all about.

Urvashi came home just as I was finishing my half-burnt and decidedly unshapely roti and the surprisingly palatable *subzi*. I told her to rejoice that she had a domestic goddess as her roomie and started to get dressed as she served herself what was left of the food.

'This is very good, Mini,' she said with her mouth full as she walked into the bedroom where I was getting dressed. 'You should cook more often. Ooh, you're trying to look pretty. What is it, a date?'

'Um,' I said, 'what do you mean *trying*? And where is that darn blue top of mine?'

'Oh, didn't I mention that I borrowed it? I did. And I left it at a friend's place when I stayed over. I'll get it back, don't worry.'

The state of Zen started shaking violently, cracks appearing on the surface.

'Okay, as soon as possible,' I said through clenched teeth as I pulled on something else and ran out, grabbing my handbag on my way.

Varun was outside the theatre, chatting on his mobile, when I reached. He smiled as he saw me. I paid the cabbie and got out, hoping that my breath was fresh and that he approved of the expensive perfume that I normally saved for special occasions such as these.

He sneezed a couple of times.

'Allergic to certain perfumes,' he said, sniffing at me suspiciously. Thankfully no more sneezes came and he decided that it wasn't my perfume after all. After this grand and auspicious beginning, we went inside. We stood about waiting in the hallway as he chatted about his day at work and the collection he was working on. I was interested in the beginning, but as the minutes ticked by I only looked interested. Five minutes to a movie, I had only one thing on my mind.

'Aren't we going to get Pepsi and popcorn?' I finally blurted when people started filing into the theatre.

'Uh? Do you want Pepsi? And now? Not during the intermission?' he asked, obviously taken aback.

'Huh? What do you mean? How can I not have Pepsi and popcorn while I'm watching a movie?'

'I guess popcorn is fine, though it would be buttered here, but Pepsi … um … not such a great idea. The sugar! And don't even get me started on the chemicals,' said Varun with a grimace, and suddenly I realised that this dream date had a fatal flaw.

Varun was a health freak.

Here he was, blabbering on about how soft drinks were meant to be toilet cleaners and how popcorn could cause water retention in some people.

I listened for a minute and then did the only thing that needed to be done in such situations.

'Hang on,' I said and marched up to the counter to order a large cola and popcorn combo.

'Let's go,' I said and led the way into the theatre. He followed me silently, looking thoroughly aggrieved.

We watched the first half of the film in silence. I chomped loudly on my popcorn, hoping that it might tempt him into asking for some. It did not work. Intermission came, and as the lights came on, he turned to me.

'Some more?' he asked as he stared into my near-empty carton. I grinned and shook my head. He went silent again.

'So, let me see, you never drink any soft drink?' I asked, in an attempt to lighten the tension.

'No,' he said.

'So what do you drink?' I asked. 'Apart from water, I mean.'

'Pomegranate juice,' he said, unexpectedly.

'That's ... unusual,' I said, biting back the caustic words that had first come to mind.

'It's very healthy,' he said enthusiastically. 'Shakti Prasad makes it for me through the day. I only drink half a cup at a time.'

'Fascinating,' I said encouragingly. 'I'm certain I would like it too if I mixed some vodka in it.'

His face fell again.

'Err, so you don't drink any alcohol either?' I voiced my horrible suspicion.

'No; the thing is, I get high with just a few sips of any alcoholic drink,' he said.

'Well, that's alright I'm sure,' I said, forcing myself to focus on his strengths. In other words, his handsome face, his incredible body. The lights dimmed, rendering this impossible.

What a strange man, I found myself thinking, as the screen blinked back to life and the characters started spouting their dialogues again.

# four

The next morning, I came in to find Shipra in a fouler mood than usual, impossible as I might have thought that would be. There was more faxing and photocopying than ever before. I was planning to spend time trying to speak to Anuradha Menon, but it was rendered impossible by the barrage of chores that were being thrown in my direction.

'She's found out about your little movie date, courtesy Prakash,' explained Mumtaaz when I finally got five minutes to myself at the Sutta Club. 'You're pissing on her tree.'

'A charming turn of phrase, my dear,' I congratulated her. 'So that Prakash seems to be omnipresent, eh? Anyway, so it's true. She really does like Varun.'

'Like, maybe, maybe not. Want, definitely,' said Mumtaaz enigmatically.

'What do you mean?' I asked, befuddled.

'Well, he has been around this company for around a year now. He speaks to her nearly everyday and stays decidedly aloof from the rest of the crowd. Personally, I don't think he has any romantic interest in her. I mean, they never go out as a couple and only talk here, at work,' Mumtaaz explained.

'But that still doesn't allow you to tread on her territory. Perhaps is reacting to your interest in him with — *he is mine and I will flood you with brain-dead work if you so much as look at him.*'

'Hmm, that makes sense. He seems very fond of her, you know,' I said, not wanting to project Varun in a bad light despite his unforgivable obsession with health foods.

'Yeah and you will pay for it,' said Mumtaaz wisely. I stubbed out my cigarette and we went back inside.

Shipra was waiting for me.

'In Avinash's office in five minutes,' she announced happily.

'Oh, alright. I will keep this ready for you,' I said, pointing at a sheaf of documents.

'Look, I know you're not a genius, but I really don't have the time to spell out each and everything for you. Both of us need to be in Avinash's office in five minutes,' she said with a smirk and walked away.

My heart sank and settled into my shoes. What could he possibly want from me? I had been doing nothing but giving the office boys company at the photocopy station. My legs turned to lead and I contemplated citing this as the reason for my absence from the impending meeting. However, one frown from Shipra and I was following her like the proverbial lamb, except this time it was to the slaughter.

'Shipra! Come inside. I have been travelling and haven't seen you in a while,' said Avinash jovially as we entered. I tried to offer him a smile and was ignored. Prakash hung about in the background. I sent him murderous thoughts via some well-timed telepathy and silently contemplated a voodoo doll.

'Yes, sir. I hope you had a good trip,' said Shipra and promptly sat down on the nearest chair. She didn't like standing, I had noticed; something to do with the extra pressure on the feet perhaps.

'Yes, yes. You won't understand much of it but things are pretty good out there,' said Avinash. To Shipra's credit, she did not wince at having her intelligence dismissed thus.

'You! What is the progress on *Azura*?' he suddenly turned to me.

'Uh, well, I've spoken to Zoya and she has promised to ask her editor if she is alright with using Anuradha Menon,' I said.

Avinash stared at me. I could see Shipra hiding a smile and looking away.

'Have you spoken to Anuradha about her dates and rates?' Avinash asked me.

'Not yet,' I said. 'I thought the magazine would need to agree first.'

'Have you fixed with *Azura* how much we are willing to pay for the cover?' Avinash asked again.

'Well, I don't know what our budget is,' I admitted.

Avinash turned to Shipra.

'Haven't you briefed her about the budget?' he asked.

'Of course she has been briefed,' she replied smoothly. 'Just yesterday I gave her a bundle of information about negotiating with publications. I hope she read it before photocopying it all and depositing it on my table.'

What? I had not known that I was supposed to read the documents. I had been asked to get them back in ten minutes. How was I supposed to read them in that time? I opened my mouth to speak but Avinash's face was already a deep shade of purple, words of rage already bubbling over.

'So not only are you incompetent, you are also extremely lazy,' he said to me coldly.

I wanted to take him by his neck and hurl him down the window with the hope that a truck carrying sharp objects was passing underneath.

I stood there quietly, slowly turning a humiliating and unflattering red.

'You don't support your boss in her work, you are making a hash of the project that you are supposed to handle and you have the nerve to come into my office to tell me all this? Get out!' he screamed. I fled.

I reached my desk and took a few deep breaths. Tears were threatening to flow out of my eyes and I looked towards the ceiling to make them flow back inside. Then I took a few gulps of water.

'Jerk!' I muttered under my breath. 'Nothing is worth this humiliation. Lardie wants me booted out, that bat from hell does not know the P of people management. I have no job description except Chief Punching Bag for Our Holy Lard there. The only halfway decent-looking guy is Lardie's friend and nuts about fruit. Why am I stuck here like a tragic heroine? I should get out! I can sit at home for sometime and I'm sure I'll find another job soon.'

Even as I said all this to myself, I knew that I would not do it. Quitting was the sensible thing to do. It was also a loser's way out.

'I. NO. QUITTER,' I said bravely.

Shipra came back looking pleased with herself.

'There you are,' she said.

'Yes,' I said calmly, hoping fervently that the eyes were not bloodshot and clashing violently with the serene face.

'Right, so you have a few months to figure it all out. The November issue of *Azura* should have Anuradha in an Angel outfit on the cover. Otherwise, my feeling is that you will be out,' she said.

'Yeah, on a prayer and a dream. Yours,' I replied, with the sweetest smile I could muster.

'Humph,' she replied eloquently and trundled back to her cubicle.

I took a deep breath. This wouldn't do. I needed to speak to this Anuradha Menon. I dialled the number of the agency that I'd heard was handling her. They informed me that she had become a free soul some time back and was now handling her career on her own. Brave, brave woman. Maybe she could give me some suggestions on how to handle mine, I thought, and then begged them to part with her number. They wouldn't.

I called up my former office to pull some of the strings that would hopefully lead to the lady. A friend of a friend knew a photographer who regularly dealt with models. He promised to source the phone number before the day ended.

Shipra went out for a meeting. It must have been something important because she did not take me along. I decided to go out for a smoke again. The Sutta Club had already heard that I was in disgrace yet again and at least two people offered to light my cigarette. I could not take up their kind offer because my cigarette was already lit, but in these things, it's the thought that counts.

On my way back I decided to stop by Tanya's cubicle. She was alone, a rare occurrence these days, given the steady stream of visitors she had, by way of suppliers making their moolah off Indian weddings. She was poring over something that looked like a fashion catalogue. Turned out, it was a fashion catalogue of the bridal kind.

'Top bridal looks of this season, available free on the internet,' she said. 'I used the printer on this floor to print it all out. I'm looting the company.'

'I strongly suspect, Tanya,' I mused, 'that you have stumbled upon your dream job.'

'Well, yes, things are not that bad,' she admitted before smiling at a cafeteria worker who passed by. 'Hello Juggu, get me two cups of tea, will you?'

'You seem to have picked up some new friends too,' I said, nodding in Juggu's direction as he jumped to do her bidding.

'Yes, that too,' Tanya agreed. 'They are kind to me, these cooks and wash-guys. There is an air of goodwill and camaraderie. I have told them that I can chop onion if they need an extra pair of hands.'

'When do you think the high and mighty will remember you again?' I asked, pointing at the ceiling with my thumb.

'I stopped asking about two weeks ago,' said Tanya. 'I am

persona non grata for all practical purposes.'

'Well, this is a great scam you have going, all play, all pay,' I said as my eye caught a colourful pile of fashion magazines. 'What is that?'

'The office subscribes to every possible fashion magazine in the world,' explained Tanya, 'and Shakti Prasad very kindly picks them up for me from the design studio. I have been looking for inspiration for make-up palettes for all the different ceremonies.'

'This is great stuff,' I said enviously. Then I told her about my disastrous date with Varun and the appropriate follow-up that came in the form of my meeting with Avinash.

'So what do you think?' asked Tanya.

'Well, normally being a teetotaller would count as a deal-breaker in my book,' I said wearily. 'But he is so good-looking!'

'Yes but then you've always been known to look for the person that lurks way beneath the exterior,' Tanya made a weak attempt at sarcasm.

'I have a feeling that the lurker is just as good-looking, friend of my youth,' I said and got up. 'I better check on the elusive Anuradha Menon's phone number. You know, Tan, I'm amazed that Avinash is willing to risk the brand as well as money by making me handle the project even though he seems so confident in my ability to screw things up. The mystery of the human mind.' Tanya nodded and waved goodbye.

Thankfully, the photographer was true to his word and delivered Anuradha's number later that day. I dialled the mobile number that had been given to me and found myself waiting with sweaty palms for her to answer. A lot depended on how this phone call went.

'Hello, is that Anuradha Menon?'

'Who is this?'

'This is Shini Mukla, except that of course I mean Mini Shukla, heh heh.'

Silence hung heavy across the phone line. I decided to try again.

'Err, I'm calling from JR Enterprises. I needed to talk to you about a cover page that we are planning to do with *Azura* in November.'

'I see,' she replied in a decidedly friendlier tone. 'What do you have in mind?'

'Well, essentially you would pose in the Angel brand of clothes on the cover and also give an interview to the magazine. During the interview you'll … uh … you know, try and talk about the brand, that is, Angel …'

'I know the drill,' she said, sounding bored already. 'Who's the photographer? I love working with Rohan Vaidya. He brings out my cheekbones.'

Predictably, I had never heard of the man of such refreshing talents. I promised to find out from the magazine.

'So, how much do you think you'll charge?' I finally asked.

She thought for a moment and quoted a number that had me gasping for breath. I squawked into the phone for a bit, and said it was a little more than what the company had in mind. 'Well, think about it and let me know,' she said smoothly. 'I'm free only in the first week of October, so if you need to do this, we'll have to work the dates around that. I'm busy with my movie, you know.'

'Congratulations and I will,' I replied weakly and then said my goodbyes.

*Well, this is going to be tough,* I thought.

When Shipra returned, I decided to tell her about my conversation with Anuradha.

'Shipra, I spoke to Anuradha,' I started. 'I discussed the *Azura* cover with her. She's interested, but the rate she's quoting seems to be on the higher side.'

She was interested in spite of herself. 'How much?' she asked.

I told her.

She thought for a moment.

'Go ahead and do it,' she said. 'It's worth it.'

'Don't I need some kind of permission from a higher-up?' I asked.

'Sure, ask Avinash,' she said with a smirk and sat down to check her mail.

I returned to my seat. I supposed if Shipra thought the rates were acceptable, they had to be. She must have done this a hundred times. Also, voluntarily going into the lion's den was not the most appealing thought.

'Nothing like the here and now,' I muttered to myself and dialled Anuradha's number again.

'Alright, I'm good with the rates,' I said when her petulant voice answered. 'I will mail you my confirmation. Also, I need to decide on the dates with the magazine. I'll call you back.'

Anuradha agreed and I was thrilled at the achievement. This was not too bad, now, was it? All it took was a lot of initiative and a lot of natural brilliance. Avinash did not know what a shining diamond lay unobserved and trampled upon under his nose.

I was convinced that the days of ignominy would soon come to an end. This cover shoot would be a resounding success, glamorous evidence of an exciting future in marketing for me. I wondered briefly if this constituted marketing, but refused to let anything prick my bubble of happiness.

As soon as Shipra went out, I rushed to tell Tanya the good news. I found her with her face resembling a constipated thundercloud, wanting to spill its angry waters on the world below.

'What's up, buttercup?' I asked lasciviously, winking at her.

'The rates for stitching sari blouses, that's what!' she said.

'Why? What happened?' I asked.

'These tailors will charge me double their regular rates in the wedding season,' she explained sulkily.

'Well, the only thing to do is order them in non-wedding season,' I said, always the voice of reason and common sense, 'you should order them now instead of waiting.'

She looked at me pityingly. 'No one can do that. What about measurements? I will lose weight by the wedding. I need to account for that,' she said bravely.

'What? Are you going to follow a diet?' I asked, not believing my own ears.

'Not just any diet, my love, the Wedding Wow Diet. Get

it? Vow, wow?' she seemed very happy suddenly. Maybe these were the famous mood swings that inordinate amounts of stress were supposed to bring about?

'What else does it entail, other than bad punning?' I asked apprehensively

'Well, the first vow is no alcohol,' she admitted, now a little deflated.

'And you're still considering it? They were right, marriage requires sacrifice,' I said.

I spent a few more minutes with Tanya, telling her all about my deal with Anuradha Menon. She listened to me keenly.

'Sounds good, Mini. You're moving ahead on the project. Maybe this is Avinash's way of testing you, you know, throw you into the deep end and see if you can float,' she said.

'Or watch gleefully while I drown, which is obviously the more likely possibility,' I replied, but secretly feeling quite on top of my game.

I did not accomplish anything else that day and went home soon after Shipra did. I spent the evening with Urvashi watching a movie on the telly and checking the phone every few seconds for messages from Varun. When nothing came even by ten that night, I started to get a little worried. I shared my alarm with Urvashi as she lay sprawled on the couch.

'Well, this is no time to act coy,' she advised. 'If he's not calling you, you should take the plunge and call him.'

'Wouldn't that look a little desperate?' I asked.

'Not at all,' she said confidently. 'When you've dated as many men as I have, you know that it is perfectly alright for the woman to make the first or fiftieth move.'

'Oh, really? Just so I know, how many men would that be?'
I checked.

'Erm, two,' she said. 'But even the latest issue of *The
Valiant Woman* says so.'

I decided that Urvashi was not to be trusted with such critical
issues and went inside to seek Tanya's help. She couldn't talk just
then, she said when I called. 'Prithvi doesn't get the importance
of a planned, themed honeymoon,' she explained briefly. 'I need
to brainwash him. I'll talk to you tomorrow.'

After spending another agonising hour dithering about
what to do I finally decided to message Varun. It needed to
be short but meaningful. Warm but not needy. Advertising
gods did not spend this much time composing copy.

*Hi! The movie was great. Lets do it again sometime.*

I pressed 'send' and then waited breathlessly for his reply.
None came. At about one, full of regret at having listened to
Urvashi's bad advice and cursing her soundly, I went to bed.
Just as I was drifting off, the phone beeped. I leapt to check
the message.

*Yes, sure!*

Well, this was short. I stared at the two words that glowed
on the small screen of my phone and tried to read more into
them. Maybe he was not the expressive, in touch with his
sensitive side, kind of man that one heard about. I could live
with that, I thought as I drifted off to sleep, dreaming about
a rosy future with him that involved many children borne of
our passionate union.

The next morning saw me taking extra care to wear matching clothes while getting ready for work. This extra care resulted in extra time that in turn created extra stress as I visualised Lardie coming at me with blazing guns and a few extra kilos of extra work. Fortunately she was out for an early meeting with a vendor. I started on the day's jobs. A little while later, Subbu came in bearing some envelopes.

'Hello Mini,' he said with his shy smile. 'This came to me by mistake.'

'You can keep it, Subbu,' I told him having taken a glance at the envelope.

'No, no, I cannot do that. You see, it is your credit card bill,' he said hastily and then caught my smile. 'Oh, I see. You joke at me.'

'So I do. I am glad the mailman messed up though. I hardly ever see you this side. Been drinking lately?' I asked slyly.

'Oh no, no, not at all. I have decided that I am not a drinking man,' he said. 'These days, I stick to cultural pursuits for entertainment.'

'Really? That is impressive, Subbu. What have you been doing?' I asked.

'Well, theatre is one of my recent discoveries in this city. My cousin Sumita works with a theatre group. I normally go to watch plays that she gives me passes for. Mr Varun also often comes there,' said Subbu innocently. 'He is a designer here. I don't know if you know him.'

'I know him, I know him,' I said, smiling in spite of my

best efforts. 'So Varun likes theatre, huh? I wouldn't have known.'

'I don't know whether he likes theatre,' said Subbu, already turning to go away. 'His girlfriend, betrothed I should say, works in the same group as Sumita. I think he just goes to encourage her in her shows.'

# five

'What a complete asshole,' said Tanya furiously and repeated the last word a few times. 'I can punch him for you, you know. No problem at all. I haven't eaten carbs for the last two days and I am looking for someone to take it out on.'

'Go off this diet, please,' begged Prithvi, and then, turning to me, 'Well, in all honesty, Mini, he never led you on. I mean he did not really try to worm his way into your life and he did not try to, how should I put this delicately, ask to see your bed-linen.'

Prithvi was right, I supposed, but it didn't help to hear it. I ordered another round of tequila shots for everyone. We were sitting at our regular pub and were discussing the latest twist in the romance that had nose-dived before it took off.

'Oh my god, do you think Mini was in lurrrve with that slimeball?' Tanya asked and violently clutched Prithvi's arm. 'I am telling you, he has that punch coming.'

'Shut up, Tan,' I said, feeling a little less than my usual cheerful self. 'There is no love involved. I am just extremely angry.'

'Why?' Prithvi asked, rubbing his arm where his fiancée had clutched him. 'Why are you angry? He asked you to come along for a movie, and he did say that he was watching films because of work and that you could tag along as you liked Hindi movies. He didn't push his luck after that, did he?'

'No, but that's probably because he was put off by my love for junk food,' I explained patiently. 'Had I told him I eat sprouts for breakfast and a slice of papaya for dinner, he would have been salivating all over the mentioned bed-linen.'

'Let me punch him,' repeated Tanya.

'Alright, did you ever ask him if he was single? Did he ever lie to you about that?'

'Well, the topic never came up, you know,' I faltered.

'Then you cannot punish him,' Prithvi finished with a flourish.

'But if we are going out as a pair, that constitutes a date which implies that he is single,' I countered.

'Not necessarily. You are colleagues; he may have just wanted to get to know you better, hang out together, share some bonhomie, that sort of fluff and pfaff,' said Prithvi.

'I didn't know you were on his side,' I accused.

'I'm here to help the cause of justice,' he declared grandly.

'I was quite certain that after a few bouts of lovers' tiffs and make-up slash make-out sessions, we would ride off into the sunset and proceed to have a dozen beautiful children,' I complained to Tanya.

'Yeah, you could have, except that we are not characters in a chick-lit novel,' Tanya philosophised. 'We are real people and this is life. The best way to deal with such schmucks is by delivering a sound punch right across the face.'

'Do you think Shipra knows?' I suddenly wondered.

'How does it matter?' asked Prithvi. 'We know and we should move on.'

'No, retribution is a must,' differed Tanya. 'The oracle has spoken. We must punish the offender.'

'Are you sure that Subbu heard right? Maybe he made a mistake. He did not strike me as a particularly bright specimen of the human race the other night,' said Prithvi.

I considered this possibility and suddenly had an idea. An idea that would establish me as the victim instead of the deranged woman seeking romance where none existed and never had.

'You know what? Varun has no idea that Subbu has spoken to me about his girlfriend. What if I ask Varun about his status tomorrow? If he comes clean, I will let it go and stop Tanya from punching him. However, if he lies…'

'Bwahahahahah,' elucidated my friend.

'Fair enough,' said the man taking a shot at being a justice of the peace. 'Let me know how it goes. We should leave now. That waiter there has been pointedly poking at his watch for the last ten minutes.'

The next day I landed at work determined to ferret out the truth about the nobility of Varun's intentions or the absence thereof. In the morning, Shipra barged in in her usual delicate fashion of a large truck brimming over with construction materials and running very late, and immediately proceeded to throw instructions at me. I furiously noted down what she was saying, trying to catch as much as I could, considering the circumstances. Circumstances in this case referring to a broken heart. Well, chipped at any rate. Definitely not as whole as it once was.

'Get it all done,' she barked at me and proceeded to ingest an enormous breakfast that had been ordered on the phone, probably as soon as she entered the building. Clearly the cornflakes diet had met with an early end. I stared at her mouth with a horrified fascination as she shovelled large spoonfuls of upma in. She liked her food.

'What?' she asked. Her tone could not be mistaken for polite.

I mumbled something about assuming that wishing her bon appétit was unnecessary and went back to my seat to call Zoya before attending to the orders of the slave-driver.

Zoya seemed to be having a better day at work and answered cheerfully.

'Hi there,' she said. 'Have you heard from Anuradha?'

'Yes, actually I did speak to Anuradha,' I replied and told her about my brief conversation with the lady.

Then I asked her if Rohan Vaidya would do the honours of capturing Anuradha's beauty and feline grace on film. Zoya said that it could be arranged. I told her the dates on which the model would be available and, after consulting calendars and diaries, she seemed to be fine with that too.

Just as I was finishing with Zoya, Shipra walked in again.

'What is Anuradha going to wear?' she spat at me.

'*Hain?*' I was my usual articulate self.

'She is not going to pose nude, is she? So you need to decide what she is going to wear,' she said, with an air of exaggerated patience normally reserved for a complete imbecile.

'Oh? Oh. I see. Of course she will wear some clothes,' I said.

'Check with Varun about our latest Bollywood collection,' she said. 'And try not to take too much of his time. He has a huge presentation coming up where he's going to show this season's designs to the merchandising team. He's very busy.'

My breath caught in my throat and seemed to lodge there for some time, indecisive about whether it wanted to go out through the nostrils or go back into the lungs. This confusion resulted in a hacking cough. While other humans may have offered me a glass of water in this situation, Shipra looked at me as if she were afraid that she might catch a deadly, uncomfortable, embarrassing and incurable disease from me, thereby proving that she was far from human. She then walked away, leaving me alone with my thoughts.

Talk to Varun? Face him after he had been such a vile lowlife? Then I remembered Prithvi's words. He was innocent till proven guilty. Well, now was as good a time as any for finding out the truth. I got up and walked to the design studio.

Varun was working at his desk, looking particularly nice in a grey t-shirt and jeans. I almost decided that monogamy was an overrated thing after all. Then my liberated and less shallow self took over.

'Hello, hello,' I said breezily. 'Hard at work, I see.'

He looked up and smiled.

'Mini! What are you doing here?'

'Nothing at all! I mean, I needed to check out your Bollywood collection for the magazine cover shoot,' I said, wondering how I could subtly bring up his relationship status.

'Oh yes, I heard about the *Azura* cover. Alright, I have some samples here. You can take a look,' he led me to a salesman rack where many garments hung in a colourful row. Varun started explaining the details of some of them to me. I decided that I needed to be completely professional and focus on the garments first. I would pay attention to the fabric and detailing, the colour and the cuts. I would push all amorous thoughts far, far away into dark and never-visited corners of my mind. Only once we were done with business would I even approach the topic of his mysterious lady.

'Do you have a girlfriend,' I blurted out the next second.

He went still for a moment.

'Why are you asking me this all of a sudden?' he asked with a sudden frown.

'Oh never mind that. I just thought I would check,' I said, unable to think of a better reason without ratting on Subbu.

'Well, to answer your nosy question, no, I'm single,' he said with a playful jab at my nose. 'And ready to mingle. And jingle and tingle too. And whatever else rhymes with it.'

Ha! I knew it. He was a cheating, lying, colossal no-good... Prithvi would hear all about this. He would hear all and then he would bow down to my superior intuition about men such as this.

'You seem very pleased about something,' said Varun and dimpled at me. In that moment I came very close to wiping out his beatific smile with the sort of punch that Tanya had been advocating.

'Yeah, it's great to know that you are, you know, available and all of that,' I said hurriedly. 'I know you are busy so I won't take too much of your time now. I'll be in touch about what I require for the shoot.'

'Sure. These will be ready in the next fifteen days or so,' he said. 'We're showing the designs to the merchandisers on Monday.'

'Great,' I said and — filled with amazement at what a rotten core his handsome face hid from the world — left the room.

I called Prithvi even before letting Tanya know about Varun's betrayal.

He picked up on the first ring.

'What's the verdict?' he asked, a little breathless.

'I hope he dies a painful death. Long, slow and painful. And I also hope he gets fat. And gets acne. And gets married to Shipra,' I said, a pathetic, sobbing mass of feminine heartbreak.

'Oh, so he did confirm that he has a girlfriend,' Prithvi deduced incorrectly.

'On the contrary, Sherlock; he quite declared his willingness to break the platonic barrier,' I said.

'But that's great! That means that there is no hidden lady in his manor!' Prithvi could be surprisingly dense sometimes.

'*Or*, maybe we could consider the possibility that he's been lying to me all this while and wanting a little action on the side,' I said.

'Nonsense. This is based on what that ass Subbu told you, and I may have stated my opinion of his sub-human intelligence on earlier occasions,' Prithvi declared.

'Gah! You just dislike him because he called Tan's beauty beauteous,' I countered with a snarl that could have passed for a grin in happier times.

'Erm, yeah, that too. But don't jump to conclusions, Mini. You know what? We should organise a fact-finding mission,' Prithvi suggested.

'Of course, Pri. Between photocopying entire libraries for Lardie and trying to get Anuradha Menon on the cover of *Azura* in Angel clothes, I have just about enough free time for a project such as that,' I said, blowing my nose loudly into a tissue.

'The problem is that you're not motivated enough,' said Prithvi. 'Listen, I've got to go now. I've been keeping six people waiting while I talk to you, and I can now see six squashed noses against the glass wall of the conference room. A disconcerting sight.'

I rang off and called Tanya. She offered her services of delivering a specially customised package of punches and blows to the offender where it hurt the most. I declined politely and told her there was a difference in opinion brewing between her husband-to-be and herself. She told me not to worry about it and said she had to get back to fighting with the caterer sitting across her desk about the best rates for paneer pasanda.

I returned to my desk and saw an e-mail from Anuradha Menon stating that she had received my confirmation about her rates. My eyes glazed over again at the amount that I had committed to paying her. I briefly contemplated a career as a supermodel, and then gave it up as too easy. I was better off doing things that made better use of my razor-sharp intellect, such as photocopying. Of course, after last time's debacle, I was now reading everything that Shipra was handing me to fax or photocopy, not knowing where she may have hidden important information.

I decided to check if Avinash was in his lair, chopping up the bodies that he may have collected over the day, to tell him that the *Azura* initiative was moving along at a brisk pace. Lardie was nowhere to be seen and I decided that it would be best to put her absence to good use.

Having trotted over to the CEO's office, I found Mumtaaz sitting in her usual place, looking her usual overworked self. I noticed that there was now a book about famous women spies over the ages lying on her desk. She looked up sadly as she saw me walk in her direction. Looking at her wan face, it was easy for even me to arrive speedily at the conclusion that things were far from spiffy.

'What brings on the blues, Mumu?' I asked with a sizeable dollop of sympathy thrown in. It must be tough, sitting in death row, waiting for the execution order to arrive.

'No excitement,' she answered unexpectedly.

'I'm sorry?' I floundered. I thought her problem was too much of it.

'Where is the excitement? I am not meant to be sitting in

a boring office! I am supposed to be a stowaway, a convict accused wrongly and on the run, a sexy secretary with a hidden agenda! You know?' she looked at me for concurrence. I nodded rapidly, not wanting to get on the wrong side of Mumu in this mood.

'Where is the action? Where is the fun? Where is the adventure?' she questioned.

'I don't know,' I admitted.

She looked crestfallen.

'No one knows. My life is a boring repetition of its own self,' she said, gloom resounding in every word.

'Look, I don't know much about stowaways and convicts,' I attempted to console her, 'but I do know that you are pretty attractive and a secretary so maybe you could work on that hidden agenda to get going.'

Then Prithvi's words came back to me and in that moment, I knew that I could help this woman full of sorrow. And myself, while I was at it.

'You know what you need, Mumu? You need a fact-finding mission,' I said excitedly. 'An exciting project that can make use of your abilities and provide you with some excitement.'

'What do you have in mind?' she asked, slightly moved.

I swore her to secrecy and detailed out the entire story of Varun's suspected and almost confirmed betrayal. Mumu listened carefully, making notes in her planner and impressing me greatly with her commitment to the cause of amateur espionage.

'So what do you say, Mumu? Will you do it? Will you find out if Varun is a blameless Adonis or a worthless jerk?'

In response, Mumu got up and extended her hand to me. I took it gingerly, not knowing what it meant in the tradition of barmy secretaries.

'I will find the truth, Mini, and I shall deliver it to you at the earliest. You will just need to trust me on this,' she said, sounding remarkably like government agent Jack Bauer in the television series *24*, when he tries to seek President Palmer's permission to supersede the law of the land, the armed forces and in some cases the laws of nature in order to single-handedly save the world and, more importantly, America.

'Great,' I said, feeling much more cheerful at having made Mumtaaz a little happier and turned to go back. Then I remembered why I had come there in the first place.

'Listen, do you think I can go in and meet Avinash for a few minutes?' I asked. 'I need to tell him something about that *Azura* project that I'm handling.'

Mumu raised her eyebrows.

'Sorry, Mini. He is busy but I will let him know if you leave a message for him,' she said.

'That's alright. I'll just mail him. I don't particularly want more face-time with him than I absolutely have to,' I said.

Mumu nodded in understanding and waved goodbye.

I returned to my seat to find Shipra waiting for me.

'Hi, were you looking for me?' I asked.

'Yes, your highness,' she said and slammed down a thick pile of papers on my desk. 'I want you to prepare a case study regarding the success of this sales promotion for me. Go through these documents and have it done by the end of next week.' She stomped off, the ground thundering in the wake of her stride.

I looked at the huge pile and grimaced. Well, I would not have too much time to mope over Varun in the next few days, that much was certain.

I e-mailed Avinash to put on record my achievement in booking Anuradha Menon for the shoot. I did not expect to get a reply so I was stunned to find a single word shining in my inbox after a minute.

'Good.'

With a trembling hand, I clicked on the monosyllabic email.

'Good', it still said.

I was good! I was better than average, I was actually good. Oh, merciful world. I did an imaginary rambunctious dance in my head for a few minutes, looking out at the world with a goofy grin plastered on my face, and then attacked the documents with renewed vigour. If I could get the shark to call me good, surely I was headed to the top in a fast-track elevator, I thought jubilantly, as I started to make notes in the margins.

My pen stopped working. Drat, my only pen too. I jerked it violently a couple of times, more because the universe expects us to do so than because I expected it to start working again. It didn't. I contemplated asking Shipra to lend me one and decided that braving the icy winds would not be worth a writing instrument. I had seen a supplies closet on my way to Tanya's desk, and since I needed a new stapler too, I decided to head there.

I slunk out of my cubicle and went to find the administration manager, a man I knew from the Sutta Club, and procured the keys to the closet. Then I went to the basement and found the tiny room that bore the legend 'Supplies' on the door. I tried to turn the key in the lock and, to my surprise, found that it was already open. I would have imagined that there was just one key to the closet. I let myself in and found someone sitting on the sole chair in the tiny room with his back to me. He turned from the computer he was working on just as he heard me come in.

Prakash!

For one split second, his face had guilt written all over it. Then it was gone so swiftly and completely that I wondered if I had only imagined it. I immediately strained to look over his shoulder at the computer screen, convinced that he was accessing porn sites. He blocked my vision by adroitly moving closer to the machine, his face once again the familiar oily mass that we knew and despised.

'Hi there, Mini. Looking for something?' he asked as if he had caught *me* doing something illegal. Unethical. Wrong, at any rate.

I dithered over how to answer this best, letting him know in veiled words that I was on to him.

I know you were up to no good, my dear. Tell all or I will. Spill the beans, o evil-doer, I am on to your little tricks. Your secret is out, buster. The game is up, my man. Dozens of confrontational phrases ran amok in my overactive brain as I tried to assess the situation. I needed to let him know that I had, in fact, caught him red-handed at … at whatever he had been doing. Surely this was the point at which my equation with Prakash would change power-centres. He would be my slave from here on, forever guilty and blackmailed.

Finally I came up with, 'Yes, a pen.'

'They're here, in this cupboard,' he said, and with one hand reached out to pick a box full of new pens while, with the other, he swiftly closed the window that he had been 'working' on. Ha!

I took out a couple of pens and a stapler and thought some more about the situation and ways to manipulate it to my advantage.

'Anything else you need?' he asked.

'Erm, no, not really,' I said and forced myself to walk out of the door.

Instead of turning back to the stairs that would take me to my seat, I headed towards the cafeteria kitchen to find Tanya and give her the latest information.

She was sitting with two women who were dressed in Rajasthani *lehengas*. I stared at them for some time. One of them saw me and smiled, revealing surprisingly white teeth. Tanya, as usual, had her nose buried in yet another album.

'Tan?' I said, a little unsure. She looked up.

'Hey,' she said, as if she was not hosting a fancy dress party in her cubicle. 'Meet Radha and Seeta — my *mehendi waalis*.'

'Err, hello?' I offered. Radha and Seeta folded their hands in synchronised *namastes*. Tanya vaguely pointed me to a cardboard box. I sat down on it. Mercifully it was not empty.

Juggu appeared with cups of steaming hot tea and a plate

of samosas. Samosas? I had never seen a samosa my whole time in that company. Tanya had sure found some fine new friends.

'Have?' said Tanya to the three of us and continued to browse through the thousands of *mehendi* designs currently on her table.

I absently dug into a samosa. Radha and Seeta too started on their tea. Just as we were finishing, Tanya looked up with something of a sparkle in her eyes.

'I like it! I like you! I think we can still squeeze down the rates a little bit but otherwise you are on,' she said. The ladies at the end of the compliment smiled. After a few more minutes of conversation, they left.

Immediately, I leaned over and said urgently, 'Tan! I just ran into Prakash doing something untoward.'

'What? How? Where?' she asked, leaning forward at the same angle.

'Just before I came here,' I said, and detailed the closet episode in minute detail.

'Well, well, well,' Tanya leaned back after I had finished telling her my story and clasped her hands to make a tower. 'What luck! To find oily Prakash at the wrong end of the law. I am most impressed.'

I allowed myself a brief, tight-lipped smile, the kind handsome detectives were always allowing themselves in cheap novels.

'What do you think he was doing, Mini?' Tanya put forward a pertinent question.

'I would settle for porn,' I said after considering the matter at hand. 'I wish I'd managed to take one look at the computer screen. I'm fairly certain it would have displayed writhing, improbable bodies in acts of consuming and lucrative passion.'

Tanya gave this theory some thought.

'Hmm, I wish you'd managed to look too. Anyway, this is still pretty good. Maybe he will keep his distance from you now,' she said.

At this I was struck by another, less happy possibility.

'Or he could decide to get me fired to get me out of the way,' I said. Tanya greeted this with silence.

'We'll just have to wait and see,' she delivered her final verdict. 'By the way, how are things with Varun?'

I told her about entrusting Mumtaaz with the fact-finding mission and then left, beginning to feel a bit gloomy about the future. I wished I had not made the little discovery of Prakash at his secret pastime. Then, in my usual decisive and proactive manner, I decided to not think about it till I absolutely had to.

I spent the rest of the day coordinating with Zoya on the shoot and filling the gaps by scouring the documents sprawled all over my desk for useful information for Lardie's case study. The day passed by, and as usual, I waited till my boss left for home and then did not waste a single moment in collecting my bag and things and getting out into fresh air.

After getting stuck in traffic for an hour and listening to the cabbie complain endlessly about the incompetence of all drivers other than himself, I reached home and let myself in, looking forward to flopping like a boneless doll on the couch and catching a reality television show that I was hopelessly addicted to. As soon as I stepped in, I realised something was wrong. I looked down to find my feet in about half an inch of water, much like the rest of the house.

Flood!

Water, as it is wont to do, had made its way all over the house, under the cupboards and the beds. There was not a dry spot anywhere on the floor. Fervently praying that I wouldn't get electrocuted, I went about the house in search of the source. Finally I found it in the washing machine. Urvashi normally loaded the machine before leaving for office, letting it do its work after which it switched itself off. The water-inlet pipe, defying its nomenclature with complete impunity, was now a water-*outlet* pipe, spewing water all over the bathroom and making its merry way all over the house. I cursed loudly in the manner of a fisherwoman and shut the tap that lent water to the machine in good faith. This was going to be hard work.

I called Urvashi first. 'I need help,' I almost wept after I'd told her what had happened. 'The whole place is flooded. We need to dry out stuff or they'll be sprouting things soon.'

'But I can't come home right away, Mini. I'm waiting for my boss to take a look at this presentation before she leaves for South Africa tonight!'

'Please Urvashi, tell her there's an emergency at home and that you need a couple of hours off,' I wailed miserably.

'I need to go, Mini, I'll call you back when I'm free,' she said and the line went dead.

I called Menaka.

'Really? So much water?' she said, expressing less than complete belief in my story.

'Yes, can you come home? I need help mopping it up,' I said, looking down at my wet feet.

'Uh … well, the thing is, I have a party that I'm taking a client to. I can't cancel at the last minute. It's a very important client,' she said.

'But what about the mess? I'm all alone here,' I said, sounding increasingly desperate.

'I'm so sorry,' Menaka made some cooing sounds. 'But think of me as being out of town. Or something.'

I disconnected the phone and burst into tears. Whatever happened to womanly bonding, the feeling of being in it together, iron-bands of feminine power, the special something that gave them synchronised periods among other things? Surely, Urvashi and Menaka did not feel that our relationship ended with putting on blue face-packs and gossiping about boys and movies and diets while they dried? I burst into fresh bawls as I realised that they were

Not

My

True

Friends

Then feeling somewhat lighter, I fetched a mop and started drying out the house. I carried the drenched carpets to the building-terrace where they would hopefully dry without getting too many pigeon droppings on them. I mopped up the house again, and finally switched on the fans to dry up the remaining wet patches. Each and every bone in my body was feeling the effects of this sudden exercise. I need to get fitter, I thought to myself, and ordered a large pizza with extra everything and free Coke for dinner.

# six

Shipra's case study turned out to be tougher than I had expected. There was data that needed to be crunched and sales figures that needed to be compiled. I found myself spending days sifting through useless junk to get to the nuggets of real information, a tip of the hat to Lardie's sadistic side, and I responded by drawing several caricatures of her with two horns, fangs dripping blood (mine) and a pointy tail. I had decided that a cruel boss was my penance for a debauched and hedonistic past-life; the balance of karma would only be restored once I had put in enough hours feeling like a particularly dim-witted specimen of the Fools Get Fired club.

One morning as I sat at my computer, reading through some numbers and sending Lardie evil spells under my breath, I had a visitor in my cubicle. I looked up to find two saucer-like eyes staring at me.

'Hi, Mumu,' I said, grateful for the break and leaning back in my chair. 'What brings you this side?'

'I have come to keep you posted. I begin my mission today,' she replied unsmilingly.

'Oh? That's great,' I said. 'All the best, Agent Mumu, may you come back unscathed from the land of cheating liars.'

'We don't know if he is a liar yet, Mini,' Mumtaaz was taking her new role seriously and would not have me jest with her. 'That is what I am going in to find out. You need to wait till the facts are established.'

'Alright, alright,' I soothed her ruffled feathers. 'Tell me, Mumu, how are you going about it? You said you'd tell me once the plan was concrete. Looks like it is now.'

'Yes, I'm going to a play tonight in which Sumita, Subbu's cousin, is performing. I am hoping that Varun will come too. After the play I plan to follow Varun; if he does meet a girl, I'll watch for what they do and where they go,' revealed Mumu pompously.

'Err, couldn't you just ask Sumita if the girl she works with is really Varun's girlfriend?' I asked. Mumu looked supremely hurt at this and stared at me, reproach written all over her oval face.

'Of course that would not help matters any. One needs to follow people and spy on them and later torture them to ferret out the truth. Everyone knows that,' I rectified hastily. The colour returned to Mumu's cheeks.

'Yes,' she said simply and turned to go. Suddenly I wished I had not dragged her into my sordid affairs. Perhaps there really was some truth to that old adage that asked us to think before leaping.

'Can I come too?' I asked after her in a last, fumbling attempt.

'Of course not. I have only one disguise,' said Mumu and walked off.

A little later I got a call from Tanya who said that she was taking half a day off to take a look at some possible wedding venues.

'It must be great to not have a boss,' I said, a touch of envy evident in my voice.

Tanya was silent for a few moments. Then she sighed heavily. 'I really think they've forgotten all about me, Mini, after having bunged me here,' she said. 'Nobody responds to my e-mails or phone calls. Asha Lata says there are no new jobs for people with my experience that can even remotely match this one in terms of the package. Of course I have no idea what to tell people when they ask me what my job profile is. I am lurching wildly between Chief Confidant to the Cafeteria Cook and Primary Giver of Directions to Lost Executives.'

'At least you are getting a lot of personal time,' I reminded her of her desire for the same at the last job. 'Any news on an apartment for me?' After the watershed event with my two housemates, I had decided that I needed to find a place where I could live by myself. Tanya's brother-in-law was a real estate agent and she had promised to check with him about possible accommodation for me.

'I think you should forget about it, Mini,' declared Tanya. 'There's no way you can afford a place on your own. Just wait it out till the company confirms you in a year's time and gives you a flat.'

'I was hoping I would be out of this place before that,' I complained miserably.

'Not going to happen,' said Tanya. Her gift for forthrightness could be disturbing at times.

'Yes, well, so I better get back to my case study,' I said as I bade adieu to my friend and wished her luck in her quest for the perfect setting for her wedding.

I spent the afternoon plodding through the mounds of information that had been deposited on my desk by Lardie. Knowing that Tanya would be out at lunchtime, I ate a sandwich at my desk, washed it down with half a litre of a diet cola and wondered if people could make sugarless things sweet without endangering half the brain cells in a person, decided that it wasn't possible and then got thoroughly depressed about it.

Water, that was the way to go, I said to myself a tad belatedly, and headed to the water cooler to fill a bottle.

Varun was standing there, wearing a lovely check shirt with lovely jeans containing his lovely bottom, filling a Styrofoam cup with coffee. He smiled widely when he saw me. I tried hard to avoid his eyes and put my bottle under the tap.

'Hey, I haven't seen you around,' he said in a bid to get into the right auricle of my heart again. Ah, cruel man.

'I've been busy,' I mumbled.

'Have you had lunch?' he asked. 'We can go out and grab something, if you like.'

What nerve! What audacity! What balls! Then I thought of something and smiled as sweetly as I could.

'Of course,' I said. 'Let's meet at the Udupi joint in half an hour. I need to wrap something up, so I'll see you there.'

'Oh great,' he sounded doubtful. 'But do you really like the Udupi joint that much? We can go to a coffee shop. My treat.'

'No, no, this is just the season for some nice Udupi food,' I said. 'Just make sure you get a table.'

'Alright, see you,' he said, and with a wave, walked off.

Heh, heh, heh, I cackled to myself after he was gone. The fly-infested Udupi joint had more clients than it could handle. The owner was reputed to swat people off if they tried to dawdle for a moment longer than it took them to wolf down their food, pay their bill and clear out. This did not include counting the change or pushing the chair back to get up. How Varun would hold a table waiting for his lunch date to arrive was delicious to imagine. Which was more than one could say for the food at the restaurant.

Retribution for my evil ways arrived sooner than I had imagined possible. I went back to my seat and saw that my mobile phone had a missed call from Zoya. I called her back. She answered on the first ring.

'Hey Mini, bad news. My boss doesn't think Anuradha Menon can work for the cover,' she burst out as soon as she heard my voice.

'No! Are you serious? What's wrong with Anuradha? Why is she doing this to me?' I wailed. This was awful. Avinash would have my head. And then claim that he'd found no brains in it.

'Nothing personal. She told me this morning that she didn't think the brand values of *Azura* — cool, courageous, comely — match those of Anuradha Menon.'

'Anuradha Menon has brand values?' I asked stupidly.

'That's what Vaishali, my boss, thinks. I think it's the part-time MBA talking. She's been saying strange things like this lately.'

I put my head in my hands.

'I don't know, Zoya. Vaishali's love for brand communication is going to cost me my job.'

'I'm so sorry, Mini. She thinks we should try to get Geetanjali Pathan on the cover instead. She seems very impressed by Geetanjali's answers at the Miss India Milky Way pageant. Apparently Geetanjali said she would use her breasts for world peace.'

'I see,' I said, not seeing at all. What was I going to do? What would I say to Anuradha? And to Avinash? Lardie would laugh till her fat sides ached. This was disastrous. My career would come to an untimely end, not that the end of my career could ever be timely.

'Do you think I can meet Vaishali myself?' I asked in desperation.

'I think so. What do you have in mind?' asked Zoya.

'I don't really know,' I said with a huge sigh. What *would* I say to her if I met her. 'But I'll get you vouchers for that new fish-spa if you can fix up the meeting. The doctor fish will nibble away at the dead skin of your feet and you will emerge, lotus-footed. Or feeted, as the case may be.'

Thus suitably bribed, Zoya rang off. I held my head in my hands for a few more minutes before Lardie's face floated in front of my eyes, snakes in place of hair, and I got back to work again. A little later, Mumu came by.

'I am going to wear a burqa,' she said.

'Oh alright, are they in fashion these days?' I asked.

She stared at me for a couple of moments, furiously judging my IQ and possibly deciding that the scores were not very encouraging.

'It's my disguise,' she explained patiently.

'Your disguise? Your famous disguise? The one that you had only one of?' I said, incredulous.

'Well, I first thought I should go as an overweight Sikh man, but I was suffocating in the fat-suit and I think I am allergic to the fake facial hair, so I finally went out and got a burqa,' she said unhappily.

'Oh dear, that is unfortunate. Because otherwise I think you would have made a perfect fat man,' I said. My caustic retort was lost on Mumu as she only nodded and went back to her seat.

Hmm, maybe I'd trusted Mumu more than I should have. The more I thought about it, the more dangerous it appeared. What if there was trouble? Mumu could get hurt.

I called her on the phone.

'Mumu, I think you should take someone with you. Just in case, you know, things get messy,' I suggested when she answered.

'I can take care of myself. I've done this before,' she declared grandly.

I was loath to ask for details of her earlier assignments and their success rate.

'I am certain you are adequately experienced. Still, for my sake, don't go alone,' I begged.

'Whom do you have in mind?' she asked.

'Tanya?' I suggested.

'No, I need to take someone Varun won't recognise even without a disguise,' she said.

'Prithvi? He is Tanya's fiancé,' I said. 'This fact-finding mission was his idea. Let him contribute.'

'Um, okay,' said Mumu doubtfully. 'I guess that should be alright.'

'Great,' I said hastily before the adventurous assistant could change her mind. When she'd left I called Prithvi and told him that the call of duty was loud and clear and he needed to answer.

'I am sure that poor man is innocent,' said Prithvi with confidence that I wished I could share. 'And I am game to prove it. Tell Mumu that I will meet her at Rangleela theatre at six.'

I promised to do so and finally decided to put aside my personal life for a few hours and concentrate on work. This was not to be. Varun called me aften a few minutes.

'You didn't come,' he said accusingly, 'and you did not answer my calls.'

'Oh no, Varun,' I said, trying to sound dramatically anguished on hearing his voice. 'I was just about to call you back. I got stuck with some critical work. You know me — work over everything else and all that. Diligent to a fault. But I hope you didn't get into trouble with the Udupi guy?'

'He shooed me off after he realised that I was holding the table, and when I tried to protest, he called for "Gangu". I did not wait to find out who Gangu was, possibly the large Udupi bouncer.'

I took a moment to suppress my glee.

'Again, my apologies,' I said, not sounding sorry in the least. 'Maybe next time.'

'Sure,' he said, sounding confused to my alert ears.

I was elated for a few minutes after he rang off. Then I remembered that I was on the verge of losing my job. I needed to prepare for the meeting with Zoya's boss. What was it Zoya had said — the brand values of Anuradha did not match those of *Azura*? Well, we would just have to prove otherwise, wouldn't we?

I was educated. I had been to a hallowed business school. I had under my belt the coveted three-letter acronym that would have won me a pretty bride had I been a straight man in the Indian matrimonial market. I had proven beyond all doubt that my only calling in life was peddling documents and presentations, providing structure to things that probably were better off without any and crunching numbers in various ways till they were battered and bruised and crying for mercy. Surely I could convince Vaishali about the merits of Anuradha Menon over Geetanjali?

If not, well then Avinash would take care of the rest, wouldn't he, I thought and groaned loudly.

'If you are done nursing your hangover,' I heard Lardie's voice from above me, 'I'd like to see the sales projection numbers right now.'

Human kindness and empathy all rolled up into one tub of lard — that was my boss for you.

'Sure, Shipra, right away,' I said. Like all well-meaning bosses looking to protect their subordinates' personal time, Lardie remembered things only at the fag end of the day, specially Fridays, ruining most evenings and as many weekends as she could manage.

It was very late by the time I finished the report that Lardie wanted and mailed it to her. When I got home, Urvashi and Menaka were both out, again. I made a solitary three-course dinner of Maggi, cola and store-bought cake and settled down to work on the presentation for Vaishali. These days I found myself opening my laptop at home much more than I would have ever imagined possible. Hard work was being forced down my throat and I had nothing more than a glass of chilled cola, a toilet cleaner according to Varun, to wash it down.

Exhausted as I was, the presentation progressed at a slow pace and soon I was yawning widely. I was about to shut my computer when my mobile rang. Prithvi! Oh dear lord, I had forgotten all about the mission that Mumu and he had proceeded on.

'Hello?' I said tentatively.

'Mini! We are done here,' said Prithvi.

'Great! What's the report then?' I asked, nervous in spite of myself, my heart suddenly picking up speed.

'Well, not so good, I'm afraid. We saw Varun at the theatre of course. He watched the play without giving too much away. No emotional cheering for the girl or anything,' said Prithvi.

'Oh, alright,' I replied, not really knowing where this was going.

'And then we followed him backstage and he met this girl, very pretty, if I may say so, and then they both went out together,' said Prithvi, sounding really guilty.

'Oh?' I said. Prithvi sounded like he had more so I added an encouraging, 'And then?'

'We followed them and they went for dinner. Mumu and I waited outside. I ate a jumbo vada-pav — which was very good, by the way. Mumu wanted an ice-gola but we didn't want to leave the post for too long,' said Prithvi. 'Plus the hygiene factor is always suspect. Mumu said she knows a gola man who uses bottled water, but then I said…'

'Get on with it!' I said, through clenched teeth.

'Erm, right, so anyway, they came out in some time and headed home. Err, together. So I guess it's true. He has a girlfriend,' said Prithvi.

'I told you so,' I said unnecessarily. Being proven right was little consolation for a future of absolute, abject misery.

'Well yeah, I think the impossible has happened. I was wrong,' said Prithvi. 'Thank goodness you didn't go out with the slimeball.'

'Hmm,' I said, suddenly thinking of a new possibility. 'No chance of them being siblings? Like in movies where misunderstandings form the crux of the screenplay?'

Prithvi coughed, a sure sign that he was withholding information.

'Talk to Mumu,' he said, and with a mumble handed the phone over to Mumtaaz.

'Hello Tsarina,' she said.

'Sorry?' I was not sure I had heard her right.

'I have coded you,' she explained.

'But of course. Listen, any chance of the leading lady being a sister to the man in question?' I asked hopefully.

'No, Mini. We also, ahem, witnessed a passionate goodnight kiss at the doorstep,' she said, trying to break the bad news as gently as she could.

'Gah! No more! Please,' I shouted. This was it, the end of my romantic tryst at the workplace. No walking together hand-in-hand to the cafeteria, no making hearts with post-its at each other's desks, no criminal wastage of office time with endless phone calls for nauseatingly mushy conversations.

'Yeah, I thought you may react this way. So anyway, we're done here. I am very proud to report that we did not get spotted — no one was even suspicious. Prithvi thinks I could be a professional spy and I'm going to give it serious thought. Listen, I need to get out of this burqa. We'll talk tomorrow,' said Mumu and rang off.

I dashed to the kitchen to counter the emotional turbulence in my life with the remaining chocolate cake. After consuming about a thousand calories in sugar, flour and butter, I felt significantly better. I could get as fat as I liked now that there was no hint of a man in my life, I decided, as I sadly wolfed down the last of the cake.

I opened the presentation and tried to start working again. I would have no personal life, no adoring boyfriend, no office romance. All I had was my work. As I led my lonely life, I would effortlessly jump from one promotion to the next till there was no designation higher than the one I was sitting on. Yes, my life would be lonely, but it would make up with the fattest possible pay-cheques, private planes and boats and some pool boys to keep me company. I would soon become a hard, polished and embittered career woman who was at the top of her game at work but depressed and loveless in every other aspect. This night was just the beginning of a long life full of hard, focused work.

Five minutes later I fell asleep on my laptop and was found snoring gently by Urvashi when she came home some time after midnight.

The next day Zoya emailed to confirm my meeting with Vaishali. I decided to work on the presentation a little more — my job depended on it and my job was all I had, now that the last shred of hope and love had been wiped out by a cruel twist of fate.

Feeling much like a tragic heroine, I ambled over to Mumu's desk a little later, clothed in mourning black.

'Thanks for doing all that you did,' I said, a guttural sound coming from the cavernous depths of my broken heart.

'Yeah!' she said happily. 'Wasn't that cool? It was a proper adventure. I can't wait to do it again. Whenever you need me to run a secret check on a potential suitor, just let me know, alright?' she said. I looked at her. She was brightly dressed in a blue top and skirt. Her eyes were shining. She was grinning. For the first time since I had known Mumu, she looked truly happy.

At least some good had come of the love-affair-that-did-not-take-off. This could be the start of something good for Mumu; perhaps she would now fulfil her destiny as a superstar spy, released from the shackles of a secretarial job that tied her to the post outside the Bat's office. I felt as if I had done something worthwhile by providing Mumu with this opportunity. I had helped someone live their dream. I had facilitated the true flow of talent.

Feeling as if I had suddenly grown six inches in height, I went first for a celebratory pee to the washroom and then to get myself a cup of celebratory coffee. I added an extra cube of sugar; Shakti Prasad had ensured that I'd developed several sweet teeth in my tenure at JRE. Anyway, who needed to watch the scales when there was no sign of a mate in sight? As I turned to go back, I almost collided into someone. I looked up to find myself snarling at Varun.

'We seem to have coordinated our breaks,' he said with a dimpled smile.

'Mmph mmph,' I mumbled and started to edge past him, not sure that I was up to staring at his handsome face without breaking it into a thousand tiny pieces and then distributing them among the poor, though what would they do with them?

'Mini, one quick suggestion if you don't mind,' he said.

'I like my coffee sweet, but I have been working out,' I said defensively (and dishonestly; I hadn't seen the inside of a gym for months).

'Huh? No, I meant about your friendship with Mumtaaz,' he said with a frown as he pressed a button on the machine to get lemon tea.

'Well, what about it?' I asked cautiously.

'I suggest you stay away from her,' he said quietly, looking into his cup of tea.

'And why would I want to do that?' I asked, now really curious.

'She is, you know, a little potty,' he said finally. 'Not all there.'

Then to make matters clearer he put his finger to his forehead and made screwing motions.

'Why would you say that?' I asked, aghast.

'I saw her last night in a burqa, following me around,' he said. 'I was…' he paused for a moment, a moment that spoke volumes of his guilt. '…I had gone to the theatre with a friend and I am quite certain she was there with a man. Then I saw her again a little later with the same fellow outside the restaurant where we were eating dinner.'

'And after that?' I asked in spite of myself.

'Nothing, I think she had enough of following me and went home,' he said. 'Or maybe she decided to spy on someone else from work. I have seen her reading strange books Mini, and I am telling you, she is a little off in her head.'

I looked at him for a moment.

'So you are certain that she did not see you take things from platonic to passionate?' I wanted to scream at him. Instead I behaved like a graceful, elegant and mature lady of the world.

'Thank you for your suggestion,' I said and turned on my

heel. 'I will look out for myself.' Then I walked away with a great deal of poise.

So much for Mumu's new career, I thought angrily as I walked back to my desk.

'Err, Mini, you might want to visit the washroom,' said a girl from Accounts as she walked by. I followed her gaze and saw that the cord of my salwar was dangling by my feet. Clearly I had not spent enough time getting my clothes in order after my celebratory pee a few minutes back.

So much for my graceful, elegant exit, I groaned as I fled to the washroom.

Decent again, I walked out of the washroom to find myself face-to-face with Avinash. Maybe the flush in the executive washroom was not working, I thought.

'Hello Saaar,' I offered tentatively and wished fervently at once that I'd not watched a forgotten-for-a-reason Rajnikanth movie the previous night.

'Gwack,' he made a sound and passed me by. I was in the process of exhaling a sigh of relief when he turned around and said. 'You!'

'Me?' I asked and then braced myself for the attack, given that I was the only one in the radius of roughly five hundred metres.

'How is the *Azura* thing going? All on track?' he barked.

'Err, mostly on track, saaar,' I said and prepared to talk about the minor problems that had cropped up along the way.

'Change that "mostly" to "all" by November or it's your

funeral,' he said. He would have perhaps said more but his bladder took some kindness on me and spurred him to more urgent tasks.

'Yes saaar, I will do it saaar,' I said. I don't think he heard me.

# seven

The presentation for Vaishali was ready. I had stayed up nights to work on it, fished out the old business-school books from their dusty cartons and even called a brand consultant that I'd known in my advertising days for some tips. He helped in introducing a great deal of substance into my presentation, recommending that I use a blue background instead of green and increase the font size of the bullet points from 12 to 14. For this contribution I was very grateful.

The presentation looked good, I thought to myself as I went through the slides. I had built a clear and convincing case for Anuradha, establishing her as the perfect match for *Azura*.

Cool: Anuradha was known to sport six visible tattoos. She was a regular at illegal rave parties and was known to have dated the Indian cricket team, individually and if some scandalous photographs on the internet were to be considered genuine, collectively.

Mmm, maybe this was too strong, but *Azura*'s content suggested that their readers appreciated this sort of borderline sadomasochistic behaviour.

Courageous: Anuradha had signed a movie with Shashank Pandey, a director known for art films that were beyond the scope of human comprehension. One of his movies included a ten-minute shot of a rice field. Nothing happens in the first nine minutes. Then a crow flies across the screen. Suicide rates regularly spiked after the release of his movies. With this stalwart of Hindi cinema, Anuradha had signed a three-movie deal.

If this wasn't a courageous career move, what was?

Comely: Old photographs revealed that Anuradha was not always the gorgeous piece of humanity that she appeared to be. Lesser women may have considered an imperfect body the will of God and moved on, but not Anuradha. She was reputed to have undergone a series of tucks where her body stuck out where it should have stayed in, enhancements where it cowered when it should have boldly declared its presence, and procedures to stop parts of her from continuing to move after she had stopped.

With this devotion to loveliness, surely Anuradha would make an inspiring cover girl.

I took a deep breath and decided that I had some valid points going for Anuradha. If all else failed, there was always the option of falling at Vaishali's feet and begging her to take on my model because my boss wanted her and whatever my boss wanted, he got and if he didn't get it, he fired people and I did not want to get fired because I needed to get a permanent position in the company so that I could get my own apartment and not have to share it with uncooperative housemates like Urvashi and Menaka and also because I had no hope of finding a decent man in my life and my job was really all I had and also because my parents thought that I had a respectable job and I did not really want to shatter their dreams in their advanced years.

I drew another deep breath and thought that it would be nice to have nicotine going in while I did it.

Things appeared positively lively at the Sutta Club. There was much hilarity in the air. Normally morose managers were slapping each other on the back and saying, 'Good one!' repeatedly. The normally reserved accountants were smirking. Even the thoroughly incompetent and much-hated denizens of the IT helpdesk were grinning, though a tad embarrassed at this display of emotion. And I could almost swear that I saw the lips of Prem Kumar, head of sourcing, twitch a little bit. I wouldn't stake my life on it of course, that would be too much, but I would wage a high bet that he had almost smiled.

I lit a cigarette and joined the fray.

'Hey, Mukesh,' I said to the nearest pot-bellied colleague that I could find. 'What's everyone so happy about?'

'Hey Mini, it was so funny,' he shook with laughter. I noticed that his belly continued to jiggle for a full eight seconds after he had stopped laughing.

'What was?' I asked again patiently.

'That Varun, he presented the new collection to the merchandising team today,' said Mukesh, chortling at the memory again. 'And it was hilarious. He said all sorts of things. Funny things, you know.'

My ears prickled at the mention of Varun. What had he

done? Mukesh continued to laugh and went on with his story.

'The presentation was being recorded, for Avinash to see later you know, and someone in the merchandising team snuck it out and we all got to see it. Oh Mini, you should have been there…'

'Can I see it?' I interrupted. Slimeball Varun, making an ass of himself. This was my fantasy come true. There was a God of unfinished flings.

'Yeah, sure. Drop by my office sometime and I'll show you the video,' said Mukesh, clearly not getting the urgency in my voice.

'How about we stub out these cigarettes right now and march on towards your office where you can part with that CD?' I asked quietly. Mukesh looked at me and finally seemed to understand the gravity of the situation. He pointedly threw his lit cigarette on the ground and squashed it with his foot. Without saying a word, he turned on his heel and started to walk back to the office. I hastily did the same.

Ten minutes later, I had the all-important CD in my hands. If I were given to hackneyed phrases, I would have even said that I was brimming with anticipation. I inserted the CD in my computer and waited for the video to play.

It was shot in the large conference room reserved for internal meetings. Varun was standing facing the camera, a glass of pomegranate juice in his hands. All the merchandisers sat around the large desk. People were talking amongst themselves. Other designers from Varun's team were making last-minute adjustments to the clothes hanging on a rack. A stack of fashion-books lay on the desk. Varun's eyes looked a little wider than usual and he was certainly looking a lot more friendly than we were accustomed to seeing him, grinning happily into the distance. He sipped nervously at his juice every few seconds.

After a few minutes, a girl from the design team who had been fiddling with a projector and the laptop, turned to him and said. 'We're ready, Varun.'

Varun took a long sip of juice and smacked his lips loudly. Then he clapped for attention. Immediately the room became quiet and everyone turned to him.

'Alright, let's see it, Varun,' said Promila, the head of the merchandising team, a ferocious looking lady in her forties.

'I believe the appropriate way to start this sort of thing is "hear, hear",' said Varun unexpectedly, and smiled sweetly at the lady whose pencil stopped in its journey from hand to paper.

'Excuse me?' she said, evidently taken aback.

'I said, I want to hear hear "hear, hear",' said Varun and giggled.

'Are you feeling alright, man?' asked one of Varun's team-mates, a gangly boy looking very concerned.

'Oh, yes, absolutely, thanks for asking,' said Varun to the boy and proceeded to slap his back, startling him considerably. Otherwise things appeared normal enough.

'You are a good kid, Sanjeev,' he whispered to his colleague. Sanjeev nodded in the direction of the merchandising head who was now twirling her pencil impatiently.

'I need to know if there is a problem, boys,' she said. 'Otherwise, let's get on with it.'

'Of course, of course,' said Varun and swayed slightly. 'I am not the one who is delaying this anyway,' here he pouted at the merchandisers. 'You people should really stop stalling. Anyway, let's show you the...' he paused for a second, '... gosh, it's at the tip of my tongue ... one moment, it's coming to me ... almost have it ... no, whatchacallem.'

'Clothes?' suggested one of the merchandisers.

'Yes!' shouted Varun. 'Clothes!'

He appeared contemplative for a moment. The merchandisers were now settling back in their seats to enjoy this unexpected presentation.

'So. Clothes remind me of something. Can you tell me what?' he threw at the crowd in general and took another large gulp of the juice.

'Why don't you tell us?' someone said.

'Horses!' replied Varun, and waited as if expecting some applause. A section of the group clapped obligingly. At this, Varun appeared really chuffed. He made clucking sounds and started to sway from back to front, possibly riding a stallion across some idyllic field, the wind in his hair and a song on his lips. His team gawped at him, wearing identical expressions of horror on their faces. His fellow designer Reshma broke out of the trance first. She took him by his arm and tried to turn him around.

'What's wrong with you, Varun?' she hissed at him. 'Such nonsense? At this time? Move aside, let me take over.'

'No!' said Varun, shaking his arm free and taking another swig from his glass. 'I am talking about horses right now.' He turned to the team facing him and watching expectantly.

'Horses,' he began contemplatively, 'are almost as good as my second-favourite animal — hippos.'

Some of the merchandisers laughed loudly. Varun grinned manically at them. Promila sighed loudly, got up and left the room, her ample behind swaying gently as she went.

'Dear old Promila,' said Varun, a touch pensively. 'She doesn't have a profile picture on Facebook because she doesn't have a profile. Being a sphere has its limitations.'

More laughter and horrified gasps.

'Yes, so to get back to what I was saying,' he continued after giggling for a full ten seconds. 'We, as members of the frashion faternity, should try to, you know, start calling models clothes-hippos.'

'I had no idea you were this brilliant, Varun boy,' called out one of the merchandisers. 'Carry on!'

'Suuuure,' Varun slurred. At this point, Juggu walked into the conference room bearing cups and glasses of different beverages. Most people had ordered tea or coffee and he placed it down deftly in front of them. Then he took the solitary glass of pomegranate juice and handed it to Varun. Varun hugged Juggu warmly.

'Thanks, man,' he said. 'I will never forget your kindness.'

'Welcome, sir,' said Juggu, trying to release himself from Varun's eager arms. Varun let go and turned to his appreciative audience once again.

'What are we here for again?' he asked them in a whisper after slugging down some juice.

'The collection, Varun, the one that you and the team have

so painstakingly worked on over the last few months,' said one of the merchandisers.

'Oh shush, Aroona,' he admonished her. 'You talk too much. Work can wait. What's important is — the birds and the bees.'

Someone whistled appreciatively. Varun got his coveted 'hear, hear' too.

'We must stop to smell them,' he advised everyone.

'The birds and the bees?' asked someone. Varun looked confused. He took another swig of his juice. Then he shook himself like a wet dog.

'The collection,' he said and walked into the clothes rack. His team looked more and more torn with every passing moment. One of them looked ready to cry. Varun patted her arm encouragingly. Then he took a dress from the hanger.

'Look at this fine piece of couture,' he said. 'It could have done Asha Parekh justice in the 1961 blockbuster *Jab Pyaar Kisi Se Hota Hai*.'

'*This* he remembers!' exclaimed Aroona, turning to the rest of her team.

'Look at the dress, Aroona,' drawled one of her team-mates. 'It's hardly Asha Parekh in 1961; more like Huma Khan in a Ramsey Brothers' production, perhaps titled "Khoonkhar Maut".'

'What?' snarled Varun. 'You, you insult my dress,' he gave the man who had dared take him on a withering look. 'Let us settle this outside, away from the ladies.'

People hooted with laughter at this. The guy who had been challenged to guns at dawn stood up. At six feet six inches and about a hundred and twenty kilos, clearly he should have been cause for second thoughts on Varun's part. But Varun was feeling invincible. He made gestures at the giant. I looked carefully and realised that he was trying to box. The big man walked up to Varun and placed a hand on his arm.

'Look here, Varun,' he said gently. 'I don't know what sort of trouble you've been having at home. But this is no place to take it out, man. And alcohol is no solution to anything, dude.'

'Trouble? I will show you trouble,' said Varun, straining to see the man's face high above his own.

'Sure you will, but now is the time to leave. Let's go,' said the man firmly, and started to take him by the arm, probably to lead him outside. Varun possibly thought that the time for the duel had arrived and, after a deafening shriek, fell to the floor in a dead faint. This was followed by much exclaiming and asking for water and calling for a doctor, as if just asking for one loudly was enough to make her materialise from thin air. At this point, someone realised that the proceedings were still being recorded on video and asked the boy behind the camera to shut shop and go home. He had created enough celluloid history for one day.

The screen went blank. I leaned back in my chair and tried hard to suppress a grin that was threatening to cause aching jaws. Well, well, well, look who had been visited by Nemesis. Our own resident Don Juan, that's who.

I was convinced that this was what fate had delivered to Varun for his philandering ways. However, it was evident that a helping hand had gently prodded fate along this righteous path.

Someone had spiked Varun's pomegranate juice.

The question was — who?

I wished I had the time to find out, but Vaishali needed to see the presentation I had made in order to save my job.

Just then Mumtaaz came running to my desk.

'It's Avinash, Mini! He's livid and he's calling you to his office right now. Hurry up, let's go, let's go, let's go!' she said and started to run back.

I followed her at a brisk pace, my heart letting me know that it was functioning well and had realised that this was a critical time and it needed to pump blood to all my vital organs. The only thing was — did it have to be so loud doing it?

I reached Avinash's office and, remembering all my thousand gods in one comprehensive prayer, knocked at the door.

'Come in,' he bellowed from inside.

I opened the door and stepped inside. Avinash was pacing the floor with what looked like a form in his hand. His face was the familiar shade of bruised purple. Prakash was there too. This was the first time I was seeing him after the incident in the closet. He looked even oilier than usual, smirking at the sound of the death-knells that were ringing in the background. I asked not for whom the bell tolls, because damn right they were tolling for me.

'Yes, sir?' I asked, at the same time ordering my knees to stop shaking.

'What the hell is this?' he screamed and flung the paper he was holding at me. I picked it up and took a look. It was the approval form for Anuradha Menon's fee, the one that I had sent to him for his signature. I looked at him askance. He glowered, clearing expecting a reply.

'Uh, this is the amount that you need to clear, sir, for Anuradha's appearance on *Azura*,' I explained, certain that there was a mistake somewhere.

'I know what it is!' he screamed. 'What the hell kind of amount are you paying her? What is this company, huh, your personal estate? You think you can squander away whatever you like? I will not let that happen, you hear me? I will not let that happen.'

I was speechless. I thought about telling Avinash about Lardie's go-ahead for Anuradha's rates and then decided against it. Lardie would no doubt deny having anything to do with this. I had only asked her verbally, there was no e-mail to support my conversation, I remembered with a silent groan. Looked like she had managed to send me to corporate detention yet again.

'Sir, I thought you really liked Anuradha and wanted her on the cover,' I began to explain.

'At these rates? Are you out of your mind? Did it cross your thick skull to bargain harder, you little piece of unadulterated idiocy?'

'So should I look for someone else, sir? I am sure a Geetanjali Pathan would do it for less. She is a very good model, sir.'

'Geetanjali Pathan? For Angel? Have you lost your mind? I want only Anuradha and no one else. Now out of my office!'

'But sir, for that we will need to pay her this amount, sir.'

'Let it be very clear — I am not sanctioning this amount. Prakash, take this moronic … thing away from my office,' he spat out. Prakash came forward to escort me out.

'But sir,' I wailed even as I started backing towards the door. 'I have already committed to this amount. We need to pay the model these rates, sir, if you are that keen on her. Otherwise, she will cancel the shoot, sir.'

'Out!' he screamed.

I fled. This was bad. Disastrous. What was I going to do now? Anuradha would not agree to revise the amount, no matter how much I pleaded. She knew I needed her.

Someone coughed behind me. I looked over my shoulder to see Prakash standing there. I turned around to face him.

'What is it?' I asked, repulsed by the sheer insincerity he radiated. The man belonged in a dodgy casino somewhere.

'Hmm, now let me see,' he said and came forward to speak in a whisper. 'You're already in deep trouble, miss. Don't make it any worse by speaking about what you saw in the closet that day to anyone.'

He stepped back. I realised that my heart was back on its pounding routine. Had I just been threatened?

'Consider this the only warning you will get, Mini. Have a good day,' he confirmed my doubts.

I contemplated jumping from the nearest window. Then I thought of my mother and how upset she would be at finding the remains of her daughter splattered all over the sidewalk. Of course she was liable to get more upset about the fact that the said offspring was still single when catastrophe struck.

*Hai, hai, abhi to bechari ki shaadi bhi nahin hui thi,* she would say. Perhaps I needed to wait to get married and *then* die, cushioned adequately by my mangalsutra and sindoor.

'How bad?' asked Mumu as I passed by her desk to get back to my own cubicle of doom.

'Pure evil,' I made an attempt at flippancy, but Mumu probably knew that my blanched face was not a result of belly-shaking laughter. She nodded in understanding and I made my quiet way back to the presentation that I was due to show to Vaishali in a few hours.

I didn't accomplish very much in the time I had left before my meeting at the *Azura* office. Lardie and the Bat flew about freely in my thoughts and I hoped that they would both meet a timely end, which was to say that a giant, fire-breathing dragon would come and eat them alive by tea-time or so.

I reached the *Azura* office well in time and sat in the reception area. I had been there earlier to meet Zoya a couple of times. The girls who worked there seemed even thinner than the last time. Size twos were crawling out of the woodwork as far as the eye could see. Much make-up was in evidence, as were short skirts and boots. Boots, in the humid Mumbai weather. Fashion required much sacrifice, I decided. I gazed for some time at the giant covers that had been framed and hung all over the lobby before a tall stick tottered over to me. I realised that it was the office assistant asking me to go inside.

I was ushered into an office, where, once inside, I was greeted by the thinnest of all the women I'd seen. A very tall, very thin and decidedly anorexic-looking woman smiled up at me, her cheekbones threatening to pop out of her face as she did so.

'Ah, there you are! Hello, hello, please come right in, I'm Vaishali,' she said. She seemed pleasant enough, but her eyes were those of a shark, not missing a single detail in my dress or appearance, assuming sharks were interested in that sort of thing. She stood up to shake my hand and I felt like my paw had been swallowed whole by a bony hand-shaking device. Goodness, did she have *any* flesh on her? She was dressed in a sari, an unexpected choice in this environment of skirt-suits, but the sari was draped way below the navel. I supposed she was working the provocative look. The belly was flat, and even in the short instant it took me to drag my eyes back to her face, I saw that a tiny diamond shone from her belly-button like a searchlight looking out for ships across the deep blue ocean.

I took a few minutes to set up my laptop and the portable projector that I had carried from office. In those few minutes, Vaishali drank a full litre of water from the bottle in front of her. She caught my glance and said, 'I drink water through the day. I get really dehydrated in this air-conditioning.' I smiled and said nothing.

'May I start now?' I asked when I was ready.

'Just a minute, let me go to the loo. All this water,' she laughed and traipsed off. She walked with a decided sway to her hips. I guessed some men would consider that sexy.

I gnawed at my nails for a few minutes. She returned to the room.

'Right, let's go,' she said.

I clicked open the first slide and started to explain my objective. She opened a small Tupperware box and started to pick at some fruit.

'Uh, I can wait till you finish eating,' I said uncertainly.

'Oh no, no, no,' she said. 'We media-people just get so used to eating lunch at our desks. Let's hear the objectives and see if they tie in with your methodology.'

'It's really late for lunch,' I remarked before I could stop myself.

'It is, I know,' she said and picked up a small piece of apple with her fork. 'I just wasn't hungry then. I had had a large mug of caramel cappuccino and two whole brownies.' Here she smiled brilliantly at me. I nodded and turned to my presentation. I didn't know what to make of this girl.

I started to take her through the slides. She nodded, all the while nibbling delicately. Five minutes later, she abruptly shut her fruit-box and started gulping down water like a thirsty camel again.

'Oh God, I am so full,' she said, and with a giggle clutched her tummy. 'I really should stop over-eating.'

I was certain by now that she was in advanced stages of some serious eating disorder. I wished fervently Zoya had warned me about this aspect of her boss' personality.

'You've hardly eaten,' I said, sure that I was expected to comment. 'Are you fasting or something?'

'Fasting? Me? Never! More like feasting,' she said with a laugh. 'I eat like a horse all the time. I normally eat butter-chicken with naan for lunch. Why, just yesterday, I was eating this huge piece of chocolate cake,' here she spread her hands to signal that the piece of cake was actually the size of a football, 'and everyone was after me — Vaish, how can you eat so much and still remain so thin? Vee, stop eating and tempting everyone! Gosh, as if a girl cannot eat her dessert in peace.'

Going by the fruit that she had discarded and the kilos by which she was underweight, Vaish/Vee had neither smelt, nor seen a chocolate cake in the last few years, let alone gobbled it down. I refrained from commenting.

'Anyway, sorry for interrupting the flow of the presentation. My bad!' she said, and I went back to presenting my slides. I explained how Anuradha, having conquered the world of modelling, was now slated to be the next star of the Bollywood firmament, how she was professional and successful, beautiful and talented, gutsy and go-getting. If my presentation was to be believed, Anuradha could have been anything from the president of the universe to the answer to world hunger to a messiah of world peace, sometimes all three at once. In fact, I had briefly considered selling this presentation to Anuradha herself, so good did it make her sound. Of course, after Avinash's decision to not pay her, this document was probably the only thing she would end up with.

I got through two more slides before Vaishali needed to go and pee again. I could not blame her, she drank more water than a bowl-full of thirsty fish. I took a look around her office while I waited for her to come back. There were a couple of pictures of herself with three rotund cats. The cats looked remarkably well-fed. Ah, maybe that was it. Cat food must be so expensive that it left her no choice but to starve herself in order to feed her pets. I chortled at my own wit and then hastily straightened my face as she came back into the room.

'Ah sorry, sorry. Listen, I must ask you, what will you have? Some tea? Coffee?' she asked me as she settled into her chair again.

'Would you guys happen to have any nimbu-paani?' I asked. 'Sweetened, please.'

She stared at me as if I'd just told her that I had embezzled pension funds from old people all over the country for the last five years, the mix of horror and distaste evident on her face. I wondered if I'd just lost Anuradha the cover issue.

'Of course, sure,' she finally said as she picked up the phone to call a peon somewhere. After asking the peon to bring a glass of lime juice she continued, 'It's just that sweet nimbu-paani is an unusual request in this office. No one drinks anything sugary in this office. People are always on some diet or the other. Everyone except me, that is. I eat everything. Sugar, bread, fat, cream, pasta — everything! I can't do without good food. I mean, what else is there in life, right?'

I didn't know how to play this at all. I contorted my face into what I hoped could be interpreted as either a grimace or a grin and she could pick what she wanted.

'Should I continue?' I asked, not sure if her bladder was ready to stay put for a few more minutes.

'Of course, please do. Time management is one of the most critical things that any manager needs to factor into her daily schedule,' she spouted these words of wisdom at me and turned her attention to the computer screen.

The nimbu-paani arrived. This presentation had more interruptions than commercials on a prime-time television show. I sipped some of my juice and caught Vaishali looking at me hungrily.

'Err, are you sure you don't want any?' I asked, feeling uncomfortable now.

'Uh, no, no, you drink that; anyway I prefer cold coffee with ice cream,' she said.

'Me too! Should we order that then?' I had no idea what was going on but I was now desperate for the woman to be full and happy before she took a call on my presentation. She claimed she ate all these wonderful foods without gaining an ounce and yet, all she had consumed was a few gallons of water and a couple of bites of fruit.

'No!' she almost screamed and then immediately took a deep breath to steady herself. 'I mean, I am really so full. Let's carry on.'

I moved on to the next slide where I had placed visuals of Anuradha in various provocative poses. Here she was in a two-piece number on a beach and here she frolicked in a forest. She pouted and invited, sultry and seductive in parts.

'So, here we see that Anuradha has been shot by the top photographers of the country. Look at her! She looks divine in that swimsuit,' I started to explain.

'I look great in a swimsuit too,' Vaishali interrupted. 'I have no problem wearing two-piece bikinis. I wear a lot of short dresses too. I can carry them off very well. And shorts. All the time.'

I stared at her in exasperation. One thing was certain. The presentation was not the key to getting Anuradha this job.

Vaishali had hardly shown any interest in it since I'd walked in. It was clear that she needed to be handled in a way different than I had originally envisaged. Academic discussions on Anuradha's merits were not going to get me anywhere. The answer to the problem lay in Vaishali's personality. If I could only figure out what, I would be home.

'Umm, yes, that's great,' I began, floundering for a leverage. 'Anuradha too is esteemed very highly for her tiny waist and...'

And then, before I could even complete the sentence, in a flash I knew that my prayers had been answered. I knew what Vaishali needed to hear.

# eight

Esteem. Respect. Regard. The answer to my question lay in that one word, except that these were three of course.

Now fairly certain that I had cracked the code to Vaishali's good books, I tentatively offered my first carrot to her.

'I'm sure you look gorgeous in a swimsuit, Vaishali,' I said, careful for any backfire that may blast my career to smithereens. 'I mean, you are really *so* slim.'

My approach was perfect. Vaishali suddenly looked interested in me.

'You think?' she asked, probably preening in an invisible mirror, and took another sip of water.

'Yes!' I ventured forth. 'In fact, when I first saw you, I was amazed at just how thin a woman could get.'

The change was truly astounding. She glowed where she had once been pallid, and positively grinned with the same lips that she had pursed.

'Oh come on,' she acted in the fashion of a coy bride. 'Surely not? I mean, really? Did you, did you, did you really?'

'I did!' I declared and nearly thumped my chest as evidence

of my conviction. 'Look at this girl, I said to myself, her waist can be cinched inside a doughnut. Yes sir, that is what I said. A small mini-doughnut too, not the large chocolate ones that I personally prefer.'

She nodded and smiled. I wracked my brain for more words that had sworn allegiance to the virtues of flattery early in life and had thereafter proceeded to dedicate their whole lives to the same. I looked at her. She was still nodding and smiling, in agreement and pleasure respectively.

'I am jealous!' I shouted. 'And I am appalled at how unfair life can be. How can one woman be carrying around the weight for two,' here I pointed pointedly to myself, so things were sparkling clear, 'and another be not heavy enough for one.' She caught the essence of what I was blabbering about and pointed to herself.

'The thin arms, the thin waist, the thin legs, the thin face, the thin arms, though I have already said arms, the thin wrists, the thin ankles, the thin legs, though I have already said legs,' I said and kept saying. In fact, I appeared quite unable to stop.

'No, actually, my arms are not very thin,' she said and held them out for examination. I peered at them closely.

'Thin!' I delivered my verdict. 'They are thin. Very thin. You could stitch a blouse for yourself out of a handkerchief, provided of course that you wanted to wear your handkerchief and were not running a cold and did not need it for another commonly known purpose.'

She looked at me, a little perplexed. She probably didn't understand what I was getting at. I myself was not too certain either.

'Thin!' I repeated in order to make myself abundantly clear.

'You know, I actually shop at the children's section of stores sometimes,' she said, the note of glee high in her voice. I grabbed at this new thread that was being offered to me.

'What are you saying?' I said and promptly put my palm under my chin to display interest.

'Yes,' she said, looking very pleased. 'They are a little short for me, of course but...'

'But you should wear them anyway,' I said. 'And to think that you are like this when you eat like a horse.'

She looked very pleased at this, not having consumed a single calorie outside of water and fruit in the time that I was there.

'You did say you eat dessert all the time, and cold coffee with ice cream many times a day and fried foods of all sorts,' I prompted.

'Yes!' she said, the lie too tempting not to be taken up as the truth. 'I can't do without my favourite foods. I like chaats too. And rasmalai. And chhole-bhature. I eat them all the time.' She looked at me for validation.

'Of course you do.' I sighed at this point. 'Some women just win the metabolic lottery and then they have nothing to fear.'

She seemed quite thrilled with herself by now. I decided to push forward my case.

'Listen, Vaishali, this minor matter of Anuradha. I understand now that she may not meet the high standards of beauty that you are accustomed to, but the thing is, she fits the bill for us pretty well.'

'Um, hum,' she said but did not rebuff me.

'I have already explained why I think she does *Azura* justice too. She will be great on the cover, I promise. Fantastic! Gorgeous! Breathtaking!'

'Maybe she will but...' she began to protest.

'Oh, please say yes, Vaishali. I will take you out for a seven-course dinner. Whatever you like. I am sure you like lasagne? How about seven courses of lasagne then? Followed by cheesecake?'

'Hee hee, I love cheese,' she said and drank some water.

'I knew you would! I just knew it. Ah, to have escaped the struggle with cellulite!'

She looked down at her skinny thighs and smiled happily at the knowledge that not a trace of the dreaded cellulite existed underneath her chiffon sari.

'So do you think you can put her on the cover as we had decided earlier?' I waited for her reply with bated breath.

I had clearly flattered my way to success.

'Well, alright,' she said and reached out to touch my hand. 'I will let her be. Geetu can do it the next time.'

I stifled a whoop and with a staid expression stood up to collect my things.

'Thanks a ton,' I said. 'I won't forget this. It was really important for me. I need to get back to work now. Maybe I will see you at the shoot?'

'Maybe you will,' she said with a smile and went back to drinking her water.

Well, that had sure been a study in psychology, I thought as I walked down the corridor on my way to the exit. Just then I spotted Zoya, walking with a notebook in her hand.

'Mini! How did your meeting with Vee go?' she asked, screeching to a halt on seeing me.

'Well, Anuradha is back again on the cover but you really should have told me about your Vee's obsession with her thinness,' I said accusingly.

'Oh, that! It never crossed my mind. Why, was it relevant?' asked Zoya, looking very surprised.

'Pretty much the only thing that was relevant in the whole meeting,' I said with a sigh.

'Tell me more,' said Zoya, having forgotten the meeting that she was presumably rushing to, so intrigued was she.

'I had an insight into her psyche that helped me save my job,' I said grandly.

Zoya goggled at me.

'What? Don't tell me you don't know that she basically wants everyone to envy her her metabolism?' I asked incredulously.

'She does, does she?' Zoya continued to stare at me. 'I always assumed the pressure to be a certain size in the fashion business had just driven her to lunacy. She imagines she eats all sorts of things, right?'

'Wrong,' I said, feeling like Dr Gregory House explaining the cause and treatment of a deadly disease, 'she doesn't imagine anything. She just wants people to believe that it's so.'

Zoya was completely dumbfounded.

'And you figured all this out on your own?' she asked me. I would not go as far as to say that her eyes were brimming with admiration and that she seemed willing to start a religion in my name, but she looked a trifle impressed for sure.

I smiled modestly and nodded.

'That's fantastic, Mini! Now you have the model of your choice back on the cover! All your problems are solved,' she said and started to walk by. 'I need to go now, see you later.'

She disappeared around the bend at the end of the corridor. I turned and started to walk towards the exit. Zoya could not have been more mistaken. My problems were far from over. I just needed to think about one of them at a time, take a bite such that I could take them in and chew on them and then spit them out.

No wonder then that my digestion was suffering.

I got into a cab and started on my way back to work. The taxi weaved through the insufferable Mumbai traffic and I had a pleasant daydream where I had an air-conditioned car and a chauffer at my disposal. I would zip around between my office, where I would be considered a manager par excellence, spending my time doing all the things that managers par excellence do, and my home, where I would live alone with no self-seeking housemates around to spoil my style. I thought about it and changed that to a loving husband, rich, handsome and doting.

I got into office and went to my desk. Lardie saw me and shouted out. 'Where have you been?' she asked accusingly.

'The *Azura* office,' I replied nonchalantly.

'Why? The deal is off, right? Avinash is not paying the sum you agreed on,' she said, the joy thick in her voice as she walked over to stand next to me.

I tried to stare her into feeling some shame for her underhanded tactics and realised that it was an exercise in futility. No guilt would ever manage to permeate that hide.

'Yes,' I said, wishing upon her a hundred years of miserable, dateless solitude. 'I had no idea that the price was actually too high since I was given the impression that it was perfect.'

'But it wasn't,' she chortled and turned back. 'So you might as well give up on the cover and admit defeat, unless of course you are planning to pay Anuradha from your own pocket.'

It had to be just my luck to be stuck in this temple of insanity with Lardie playing the high priestess.

'I heard about Varun's novel and refreshing approach to presentations,' I said calmly. That got the spring out of her step as expected. She scowled at me.

'Someone spiked his juice,' she said, 'and that someone will be found out and punished, that much I can assure you.'

'We'll see,' I said and opened some files pointedly on my computer. She hmphed and went back to her desk, looking alarmingly unattractive in a green kaftan top, I thought charitably to myself.

As expected, she punished me with more work. The case study that I'd prepared for her came back bearing more remarks than a scantily-clad woman evokes walking past a few dozen construction workers. I sighed as I realised that there would be no respite for me for a long time to come and got back to work.

At about four, Lardie picked up her bag and left. The fresh chocolate croissants at the nearby French bistro called out to her nearly everyday at tea-time and she proceeded to do their bidding. As soon as she left, I went down to the basement to meet Tanya.

'How did your meeting go?' she asked, looking up from a thick pile of fabric swatches when she heard me.

'Pretty good. I cracked that Vaishali open,' I told her proudly.

'I hope you mean that in a good way,' she said and put away her swatches. 'For the *lehenga*,' she explained when I looked at them questioningly. 'Velvet and silk, kalidaar and A-line, zari and zardozi, decisions and decisions.'

'You seem to have it under control,' I remarked.

'Hmm, I guess I'm getting the hang of it. Anyway, tell me more about the meeting,' she said.

I gave her the gory details of all that had transpired. She seemed very proud of me.

'Well done, now Lardie will be burning up when Anuradha does appear on the cover,' she said.

'The cover is still in the far distance, Tan. I have no idea how to pay Anuradha. But yes, Lardie appeared far from pleased. I dropped a little remark about Varun's performance. Did you see that video? Oscar moment and what not, eh?' I asked.

In response, Tanya looked both sheepish and proud.

The truth dawned. I stared at her in unmitigated horror, my breath stuck in my throat.

'Oh my god, Tan,' I moaned. 'You spiked his juice, oh nooooo...'

'You don't have to call me god when...' she started.

'Shut up!' I hissed, she petered out. 'Did you really do it?'

'I did. But I cannot take full credit for the successful implementation of a brilliant scheme, assisted as I was in my endeavour by a team of supportive and efficient helpers, though of course they had no idea they were serving me,' she said mysteriously and grinned.

'What have you done, Tan? They will find out in no time and then you won't even get time to collect all your wedding paraphernalia, so quickly will you be booted out,' I said miserably, a variety of dire scenarios flashing through my mind.

In response, she continued to look very smug.

'How did you manage it anyway?' I asked, curious in spite of myself.

'A simple and yet brilliant plan, if I may say so myself,' she said. 'I asked Shakti and Juggu to err, let me help out in the kitchen. You know I occasionally do that, right, specially when pav bhaji is being made and vegetables are chopped by the kilo? After that it was only a matter of time before I figured where the juicer was kept. A dash of vodka was all it took. Why, vodka, you ask? Why, it has no odour, you see, and is easily disguised.'

'Oh dear lord, that means Shakti and Juggu may lose their jobs too,' I concluded with yet another moan.

'Not at all,' she said complacently. 'They had no idea about what happened. They were unsuspecting comrades at best. I take full credit for the planning, implementation and execution of the entire plan.'

'Plan? Smuggling alcohol inside office? Inebriating the staff? Using the office kitchen to further your own motives?' I asked in a horrified voice.

In response, she took an elaborate bow without getting up from her chair.

'But why, Tanya, why? I thought you were busy enough with the wedding preparations, even if you don't have any work to keep you occupied. Why this?' I asked, looking over my shoulder for security guards that may be hunting down Tanya even as we spoke.

'I thought the motive was clear enough,' she replied in a remarkably unperturbed tone. 'He played the ladies' man with you. I played him. Tit for tat, if you know what I mean.'

'Boy, I am so touched,' I wailed. 'Once you announce the motive to the court martial committee, I will be sent packing too.'

'Yeah, that is a possibility,' admitted Tanya with a nod, not really seeming too perturbed by that either.

I groaned for a full minute while an unrepentant Tanya leafed through *A Hundred and Twenty Ways to Looking Beautiful and Unlike Yourself On Your Wedding Day*, a thick tome devoted to bridal make-up.

'I think you could be a little grateful, you know,' she said after I had finished expressing my dissatisfaction. 'I did it all for you. No one will ever mess with you after they realise who is watching your back.'

'My back, the one you are so carefully guarding, will bear the large imprint of Avinash's boots and it will be seen walking into the Twilight Zone of Destroyed Careers,' I said, and with a moan got up to return to my own cubicle to await execution orders.

'That's your problem, Mini,' Tanya called after me. 'You really need to look at the brighter side of life.'

I didn't bother replying.

When I got back, there was an e-mail from Anuradha, asking me to confirm the dates for the cover shoot. If only she knew the lengths to which I had gone to make this happen. I considered replying and then the ferocious face of Avinash floated past the eye of my mind. It was being pursued by my salary cheques for the next few years, sporting tiny wings and all proceeding on their way to Anuradha's bank account. I let out another heart-rending whimper and put my head down on my desk. This was so much tougher than I'd imagined possible. There was only one thing to be done now, the remedy that all hard-nosed career women need when they are faced with unforeseen tribulations. I picked up the phone.

'Mommmmmmmmmmeeeee,' I wailed and then proceeded to tell her about the days of collective misery that had made their way into my life.

I allowed my mother to soothe me for the next few minutes. She was openly and blindly supportive in the tradition of mothers. She soundly cursed all and sundry who were torturing her daughter thus, and hoped that the afterlife would involve creepy-crawlies in open wounds for each person who was making her child work for her money. As always, I felt significantly better after I had ranted to her. As always, the moment I felt better she began detailing her plans to get me married by the end of the year. I hastily told her that I needed to speak to my father.

'When are you coming home?'

'Soon, Pa. I have a lot of work right now.'

'Mom looks worried.'

'Mom wants me married.'

'No harm there, except for one thing.'

'What's that?'

'No one can be good enough for you.'

'I know, father, and I think the menfolk know it too.'

'How is work?'

'Depressing.'

'Win this battle and then move on.'

'I know. Bye.'

'Bye.'

Shakti Prasad put a cup of tea on my desk. I thanked him and looked for tell-tale signs of stress on his face, given Tanya's recent adventure in his kitchen. He looked perfectly happy.

'Erm, Shakti Prasad, did you hear about what happened to Varun?' I asked hesitantly.

'Yes, madam ji, in the middle of the presentation, Varun sir got drunk,' informed Shakti Prasad, succinctly and piously.

'Do you know how it happened?' I asked, glad that he was so innocent.

'Haan, of course. Someone mixed vodka in his juice,' said Shakti Prasad and started to leave.

'Any idea who did it?' I asked.

'No,' he said and walked off with his tray of steaming cups.

I heaved a sigh of relief. At least, Shakti Prasad and Juggu could not be called accomplices. Once Tanya and I were convicted felons, maybe they would bake and bring us cakes with concealed saws.

Since time flies when one is having fun, I somehow trudged through the excel-sheets that Lardie had left me to go through (without explaining why) for the next few hours. At about eight I got a call from Tanya asking if I was ready to leave. I was surprised to find her in office at that hour. She normally left with the clock-watchers, when the clock struck five-thirty. I asked her to come up. She came bearing a cake box.

'I thought I would check if you're still angry,' she explained when I asked her why she was putting in overtime, 'about my tryst with Varun's destiny, I mean. Also, the cake guy could come in with samples only after shutting his shop.' She opened the box and I gasped at the various cakes that sat there. Pink cream with little red hearts adorning it, soft chocolate with a moist vanilla centre, cookies and cream, pista and nuts — there must have been twelve varieties of cake in there.

'I thought you might like it,' she said.

'I do, I do, I do,' I said and started to hunt for a fork in my desk. I am not the sort of person whose every action is controlled by desserts, but they definitely had an impactful presence in my life.

'I thought we could go to my place to finish it,' she said.

'Alright then, look sharp!' I replied, and shoved some stuff into my handbag, eager to leave.

We left the building and started to walk towards the parking lot. Tanya had borrowed Prithvi's car, she said, and had parked it in the office's outdoor parking lot. The parking lot was gloomy like parking lots are and should not be. Tanya led the way to where Prithvi's small red car stood awaiting instructions and fished in her handbag for the keys. Suddenly out of nowhere, we heard a voice.

'I know you did it!'

I jumped out of my skin and screamed blue murder simultaneously. Tanya had greater presence of mind and held out her sunglasses to protect us from the intruder.

Prakash stepped out of the dark.

'It's me,' he stated the obvious.

'We can see that,' I said crossly. 'What are you doing here?'

'Well, I just thought I'd come over and have a friendly chat with both of you,' he said, oil dripping from every word. He might as well have been a potato chip.

'As I said before you, ahem, got out firearms to attack me,' here he shot a look at Tanya's Gucci sunglasses, which she hastily shoved back inside her bag. 'I know what you did.'

Tanya and I exchanged uncomfortable glances.

'What did we do?' Tanya asked, a touch defiant.

'The little matter of polluting an innocent designer's even more innocent juice is what I am referring to. Perhaps I did not make myself clear,' he said, 'you infiltrated Varun's juice.'

Tanya looked at me. I looked at my shoes.

'Who said so, I'd like to know,' said Tanya, still hoping that blatant lying would help her slip out of the situation.

'I, uh, interviewed Juggu and Shakti Prasad about exactly what transpired in the kitchen that day. He mentioned that you had access to the juicer,' Prakash smirked at us.

'That doesn't prove anything,' shouted Tanya. 'I didn't do anything.'

'Well, I'm asking Avinash to set up an investigation into the matter tomorrow,' said Prakash. 'Maybe they will be able to get an admission out of you. It may even involve the police.'

'Hah!' said Tanya. 'The police have greater responsibilities. They need to chase robbers and fight criminals. Or accept bribes at any rate. I am just a piddly juice-spiker.'

'So you do admit you did it,' said Prakash smoothly.

'Maybe I did. What's it to you?' said Tanya, now itching for a fight.

'Well, it's actually fairly simple. I look after matters of peace and justice in this company and I wouldn't want anyone to go about poisoning our designers and jeopardising our presentations. So keep to your little hole in the wall in the basement and don't crawl out.'

I hadn't been much use till then, I was too overcome by Prakash's onslaught, but I finally managed to recover my voice. 'What what what what what,' I said and then for impact added, 'what what what?'

Tanya, too, bristled at what Prakash had said. 'Are you threatening me?' she sought to clarify from the grease can in front of us.

'Well, let's just put it this way — I foresee immense misfortune in your future if you decide to disobey me,' he said slickly.

'Well, I have news for you, soothsayer,' said Tanya and waved an admonishing finger in his face. 'I foresee a beautiful, talented and spirited girl walking into the CEO's office and telling him all about your dirty secret from the supply closet if *you* don't keep *your* mouth shut about the juice episode.'

Prakash looked confused for a moment.

'That girl would be me,' Tanya clarified further.

Prakash's face blanched. He looked at me. I was discovering the meaning of existence in my shoes and could have looked at them for all eternity.

'You told her,' he accused me.

'Well, yeah, but she won't tell anyone, I promise,' I said, looking at Tanya for agreement.

'I won't if he won't,' observed Tanya calmly.

Prakash stared at us for a few seconds and then turned on his heel and walked away slowly. Soon he had disappeared from sight.

I heaved a sigh of relief and turned to Tanya. She looked poised, like she always did when she had successfully blackmailed someone.

'Thank goodness he's gone,' I said as we got into the car. 'But Tanya, we don't know what he was doing in the supply closet. Obviously he was hiding something, but if he decided to tell on you, we really don't have anything to retaliate with, do we?'

Tanya put the car in gear and backed out of the parking lot.

'We know that but he doesn't. He thinks you saw more than you did the other day. Now all we need to do is find out his dirty secret and I can have him on a tight leash for the rest of our time here.'

'But how will we figure it out? Let me make myself clear right now, I am not going to pursue him into closets.'

The car weaved in and out of the Mumbai traffic. Tanya had spent all the rage that she normally reserved for the road and was being quite the docile driver. We stopped at a traffic signal.

'You won't, but we know someone who would,' said Tanya and smiled.

# nine

The day of the shoot was drawing closer and I still had no idea where Anuradha's money would come from. Avinash had not said anything about it, and other than fearing that my gratuity would go towards clearing the payment, I did not know what else I could do. I had not spoken to Anuradha about the money, but I figured that unless I did it, I would have no model for the cover. After dithering about my course of action for a few days, I called her one morning. She sounded sleepy.

'Anuradha? Hi, it's me, Mini. I wanted to talk to you about the *Azura* shoot,' I began.

'Hey Mini, sorry, I was out till late last night,' she said. 'We were shooting the last day of the annual calendar for Viper's Venom beer.'

'That sounds … interesting. Listen, about your rates,' I said.

'What about them?' she asked. 'I know I have undercharged you but hey, I'm working without an agency these days so that's alright. You were just lucky!'

I gulped.

'Actually, Anuradha, I was hoping that you would settle for a little less than what we originally agreed upon.'

'What? Absolutely not,' she said, suddenly wide-awake and every bit the shrewd businesswoman. 'I do not negotiate on rates after I receive a confirmation from my clients and I do have one from you, Mini. On mail, may I remind you?'

'Ah, augh, yes, of course. I just wanted to check,' I said, turning from human to chicken.

'No check, only cheque. I wish you'd just let me know whether you want me to do this or not,' she whined. 'I have already refused other offers, you know, because I had given that date away.'

I thought of Avinash again. He would strangle me if Anuradha did not appear in Angel clothes on *Azura's* November cover and Anuradha would choke me if I did not pay her what I had agreed to.

In any case, death by asphyxiation seemed to be my destiny.

I might as well get the cover out before that.

'Ha ha ha,' I trilled into the phone. 'Of course you need to do the cover for us. I was just, checking, you know. Times are hard financially and all that. Anyway, see you at the shoot.'

She hmphed and disconnected the line. There was nothing for me to do now. I *could* steal something precious from Avinash's office and try and sell it to pay Anuradha, but with Tanya already charting out a criminal course for us, that seemed a tad inadvisable.

The other thing I needed to arrange was what she would wear. I had obtained Anuradha's vital statistics and I needed to organise the clothes that would be used at the shoot. There was only one problem with this — I would need to talk to Varun. He was in charge of the Bollywood collection and would need to authorise the release of the clothes. One day, when I could no longer posspone it, I gathered my courage and went to see him. He was sitting in his studio, deeply immersed in his work.

'Hey Varun,' I called out.

'Mini!' he turned and got up to ... what ... hug me? I took a step back and held out my hand instead.

'Hello, hello,' I said, trying to sound jovial while all the time I had the awful image of Tanya mixing drinks, two horns on her head and a pointed tail peeking out from under her skirt.

'Hello to you!' he dimpled at me. 'Where have you been? I don't see you around at all and Ships says that you're not really busy either.'

'She would,' I mumbled darkly to myself. After all the time I had spent on Keep Self Out of Shipra's Hair projects, I had developed frightening dark circles under my eyes and consequently had damaged my chances of finding a suitable groom before hitting thirty. And after this immeasurable sacrifice she had the gall to tell Varun that I was hardly working.

'Um mum, gah bah,' was my intelligent reply to the smiling man in front of me.

'Anyway, come here, sit down,' he said and pulled out a chair for me. I sat down and held my notebook out in front as some sort of defence.

'I'm here to discuss the clothes for the *Azura* shoot,' I said.

'Listen, did you hear about my juice incident?' he said, sounding very concerned. 'Though, what am I thinking? *Everyone* heard about my juice incident! Terrible, huh?'

'Yes, yes, terrible. Horrible, in fact. Wicked,' I said and hastily opened my notebook. 'Now here's what I need. These are the model's measurements... I need jeans and tees. Some bling is always a good idea for shoots, I'm told...'

'I wonder who did it. I know Juggu didn't,' he said in a contemplative fashion.

'No one did it!' I said before I could check myself. He stared at me.

'Well, I mean, whoever it was, I'm fairly certain they'll be caught soon,' I tried to amend my words. 'And then, then no punishment will be too severe for the guilty party...'

He continued to stare at me.

'...whoever they may be.' I trailed off into silence.

'Wow!' he said and then stared at me some more. I began to feel uncomfortable under his unwavering gaze.

'I had no idea,' he whispered, 'that you cared so much.'

He reached out for my hand.

'Thanks Mini,' he said with some mistiness inexplicably showing in his eyes. 'This means a lot to me.'

'Oh ho ho, what rot and all that you talk, *hain*, whatnot and sweet nothing schmuthing, sweet sorrow, parting and go-carting...' Somehow, I managed to force myself to shut up. To be honest, I felt a little drunk. Things were moving way too fast.

'Now I know,' he said, 'that you actually deeply care. You do!' With that he got up and picked up a catalogue.

'Here, take a look and let me know which designs you need for your shoot,' he said, handing it to me. I took it meekly and got up to leave. He took my hand.

'Take care, won't you?' he said, his puppy eyes looking at me with something resembling infatuation.

'I will, hee hee,' I said and skidded out.

I called Tanya when I reached my desk.

'I am armed with pepper powder,' she informed me when she heard my voice, 'in case Prakash decides to play rough. And I have asked Juggu to deliver some garam masala to my desk too. Don't worry, Mini, I will take care of you!'

'I wish you wouldn't' I snapped. 'I have just got back from Varun's studio.'

'Oh shit! Does he know that we did it?' she asked, concern evident in her voice.

'First of all, *we* didn't do it, *you* did! And second, he doesn't know that we did it. On the contrary, he thinks that I care deeply about him, and what's worse, he's reciprocating!'

'But I thought you liked him!'

'I thought I did too. But he gets drunk on one drop of vodka and has a girlfriend. And therefore I now find him more irritating than amour-worthy.'

'Ahh, so you changed your mind, eh? Maybe you should tell him that you know he has a girlfriend,' Tanya suggested.

'Sure, so that he can put two and two together and come to the conclusion that Mumu and Prithvi trailed him and that you tried to poison him on my behest to get back at him? I will definitely get fired then!' I wailed.

'Hmm, it is a complicated web that you've woven,' said Tanya with all the wisdom of a particularly gifted sage and rang off. I wanted to throttle her with all my might. Instead I picked up the catalogue and started sifting through the numerous designs that were featured there. A few distracted halter-tops and some pensive Capri pants later, I gave it up for some other work. This shoot would be the death of me. There were not too many days left and I had already had enough stress to warrant a three-week holiday in the Bahamas. Or Bhilai. Just far, far away from this madhouse.

Mumu sidled over to my desk a little later in the day.

'I believe Prakash threatened you and you responded with a counter-threat,' she whispered, making me jump out of my skin.

'It was not me. It was that ass Tanya,' I said.

'Yes, Tanya mentioned that you seemed to be assessing the exact amount of dirt on your shoes,' said Mumu helpfully. 'I have nothing but the highest regard for Tanya's ability to bring back equilibrium in the world.'

'She is a borderline criminal and you are only encouraging her further. And my shoes are spanking clean, I will have you know,' I said and pointedly turned my back to her, in a manner of speaking.

'Maybe,' she said in a non-committal tone and then edged closer. 'I have a purpose to my visit.'

'Gah! I knew it!'

'Tanya tells me that you need to prise a secret out of Prakash,' she said, her eyes gleaming.

'Well, yes, Tanya believes that counter-blackmail is the only way we will both get to keep our jobs,' I said.

'She's right and I offer my self for the job,' she said. 'I think I should be a cinch for this assignment after the resounding success of my last project.'

I permitted myself a hollow groan inside. I might as well have bought front page space in the *Times of India*, so discreet had the investigators been while tailing Varun and his girlfriend.

'I guess I don't really have a say in the matter,' I said.

She looked at me in silence, confirming my suspicion.

'Well then, what do I say, go ahead and do it,' I said, hoping my resignation held the right mix of hurt and bewilderment.

She grinned at me and walked away. There was no knowing what would emerge from this.

I went back to my work. After some time, Lardie walked over to scream at me for botching up the report she had given me to write, her entire strategy for that product, and from how she sounded, I had possibly disrupted the system that caused the change of seasons in the world. After giving me a thorough verbal spanking, she split for the day. I was getting almost immune to her tantrums, but it was still far from pleasant to be called a cretin with minimal intelligence, a nincompoop who added new dimensions to the word stupidity and a jackass who should have paid the company money to let her work there, all in one short breath.

I let out a sigh after she had left and looked through my plan for the *Azura* shoot once again. So far, it looked like I had everything on track. I just needed to figure out a way to pay Anuradha and then we would be home free. At least there was no advance payment involved. Zoya had even confirmed that Rohan Vaidya, the photographer who had the remarkable talent of bringing out Anuradha's cheekbones, would be doing the shoot. I had decided on and marked out the clothes that Anuradha would wear for the shoot in Varun's catalogue. I needed to get fittings done, for which Zoya had arranged a dummy model, a sort of stand-in for Anuradha. All I needed to do was get to the *Azura* office with the clothes. The photographer would also attend the meeting and finalise the concept for the cover. I wished I had someone a little more senior to come with me. These were all important people and I was a novice who knew nothing about the right things to say and do. Lardie was out of the question. I might as well have asked a barracuda to give me lessons in corporate excellence. Avinash? I giggled hysterically to myself. Yes, this was the deep end of the pool and if I could not teach myself how to stay afloat, I would meet my watery grave very soon.

I avoided Varun over the next few days and stole into the design studio early one morning to keep the marked catalogue back at his desk with a carefully worded note addressed to him.

*V!* (it said)

*Have marked the clothes I need for the shoot. Please get them in a size medium. Will come by to collect them on Tuesday. Hope that gives you enough time.*

*Mini*

I thought that was as neutral as it could get. I picked up a flower-vase that stood on one of the tables nearby and used it to hold down the note.

The day of the garment trials was almost upon me! I needed to think fast and straight, stay focused and deliver the goods. I kept prepping myself to believe in Mini Shukla — a tough act given that no one else did. I needed the support of my friends in my hour of need. Speaking of which, I had not seen Tanya for a few days, so occupied had I been with my own project. I had even been eating lunch at my table, playing a few furious games of Solitaire to relax myself while I prepared for battle. I decided to go and check on her one evening. It was just as well that I did, because I found her sitting under a shamiana.

I stared in silence at the colourful canopy covering her cubicle for a few minutes. The distinctive red and yellow pattern on the fabric stood out for about five miles in each direction. Tanya, looking very much at ease in her surroundings, was making a list in a notebook.

'What is this?' I finally blurted out.

'Oh hello there, I haven't seen you in ages,' she said, smiling broadly.

'What is this?' I touched one wall of the shamiana and sat down. Then I noticed that I was sitting on something that remarkably resembled the type of opulent thrones normally reserved for brides and grooms at their wedding reception. Tanya was also seated on a similar chair. Her throne was red and blue while mine was blue and gold.

'And what are these?' I pointed to the chairs.

'These are the chairs that I have short-listed for the wedding. I still need to decide between these two. And this of course is the shamiana. Do you like it? A little traditional, maybe, hmm?' she said and seemed lost in her thoughts for a second.

'Shamiana? Wedding chairs? What the hell do you think you are doing, Tanya? This is not some furtive meeting with a caterer. This is taking things to a different level altogether. You are sticking out like the sorest thumb in a long history of sore thumbs. They will kick you out! What are you doing?' I paused for breath.

She smiled. 'Well, I have been sitting under the same shamiana for three days now and not a word has come from anyone,' she said. 'I could invite my *baraat* in here, they could come with the biggest band and a horse and no one would say anything.'

'But it's been months since this has been going on, Tanya. How long can you be ignored like this?' I asked, a little scared that this isolation was causing my friend to become a little deranged. Did she have any idea how ridiculous she looked sitting under all that patterned fabric?

'I spoke to someone in HR. She doesn't know anything either. Apparently the CEO's orders were to make me persona non grata in this office, till further orders. They can't make any changes to my status till they hear from him again. After what happened to John Peters, everyone is petrified of approaching him and they are just letting sleeping dogs lie and jobless Tanyas be jobless,' she explained.

'This cannot be good for your career,' I said doubtfully.

'Maybe not, but it is great for my wedding,' she said cheerfully and pulled out a stack of sample wedding cards. 'Take a look and tell me which one you like. Prithvi refuses to have anything to do with all this anymore.'

I hung about for some time helping Tanya select a suitable card. Then I left her to modify the words in the invitation. I didn't want to hurt her feelings but I was feeling rather silly, sitting under her shamiana. I walked absent-mindedly to my desk and spotted someone putting something on it. He turned around as he heard me approach.

'Varun! Erm, hey, what are you doing here?' I said as nonchalantly as I could. Then I caught sight of what he was doing and nearly threw up all over him. It was a purple carnation with a small card attached to its stem.

'For you,' he said, smiling at me.

'Gulp,' I said.

'Say something,' he said.

'Why the flower?' I croaked up at him.

'I got your note,' he explained patiently.

'My note? The one about the clothes?' I said. He nodded. How the hell could that note have inspired him to give me a flower, I wondered. Then I had visions of Lardie changing that note for something a little more passionate, but then dismissed it recalling that Lardie quite liked Varun herself.

'Err, hey, thanks. This is very generous of you,' I babbled, 'though a trifle unexpected, if you know what I mean. But I am in receipt of your generous gift, of course.'

He waited for me to wind down. I did.

'You called me "V"! I love that, I do,' he said inexplicably. I stared at him. I had thought 'V' would sound even more impersonal than 'old chap'. Clearly I had been mistaken.

'What does a purple carnation mean anyway?' I asked him with a nervous laugh.

He looked a little confused at that.

'Well, same as what you meant when you left the vase containing the purple irises on top of the note. Purple stands for passion. And desire,' he replied, with the lost lamb expression back in his eyes.

'Oh dear lord,' I swore under my breath. Trust me to not carry a cabbage with me to hold down notes.

'Well, well, well,' I said heartily and gave him a friendly pat on the back. 'It's been great catching up with you.' To my dismay, my friendly gesture seemed to go down as a gesture of the passionate kind and he gave me another meaningful look.

'Anyway, see you later, old chap,' I said and shooed him out.

He went away, whistling 'Save the last dance for me' under his breath. I sat down heavily and stared at the sodding purple carnation. I needed a cigarette to tackle this new development. I went out to join the Sutta Club for a smoke and some gossip. Mumu was there too, apparently collecting information on Prakash. I spent about ten minutes there, chatting with my smoke buddies and, feeling much better, sauntered back to my cubicle. For the second time that day I found someone there already.

Lardie, holding the purple carnation and looking every bit the Greek Goddess of Rage.

'What is this?' she asked me through clenched teeth.

'A purple carnation,' I said, wilting under her furious gaze.

'That means — Varun and you...' she said. I waited for her to finish but apparently that was all she had to say.

'Augh, no! I mean, not that it is any business of yours, but no, no, no, not at all,' I blabbered.

'Not my business! Not my business?' For a sickening moment I thought she would have a seizure. 'You and *my* Varun! Not my business?'

'Look, Lar ... I mean, Shipra. There's nothing going on between us,' I tried to calm her down. 'It's just a giant misunderstanding.' For a moment I contemplated telling Shipra about Varun's secret girlfriend. Then I decided against it. I did not want to meet an untimely end here, in this despicable office.

'There's nothing,' I finished.

'There better not be,' she said, waving a murderous finger in my face, 'because if there is, you are toast.'

She stormed out, still shaking with rage, throwing the purple carnation on the floor as she went. Then she remembered something and turned around.

'And not a word about this ... talk ... with him, you hear? Otherwise, I promise you, you will not stay in this office for a minute longer than it will take you to pack your sorry belongings,' she stated and went back to her desk.

Well, threatening colleagues was apparently a regular way of life at JR Enterprises. Land at work, order coffee, crunch some numbers, threaten Mini, take a break.

I shook myself like a wet dog. Threats, intrigue and lies all around — all part of a day's work. One had to move on. I sat down and booted my computer. I stared at it unseeingly for a few minutes. Things were spiralling out of my control. I needed to have some sort of plan of action to tackle unfriendly people as they jumped at me with new unpleasant surprises everyday. I took out a piece of paper and started writing.

*Lardie*

Problem: (*I thought about where to start and then wrote*) Likes Varun. Will kill self if catches self with Varun.

Solution: Avoid Varun at all costs.

*Varun*

Problem: Under mistaken impression that self likes him. Self doesn't like him (anymore). Has stashed away girlfriend. Cannot be told off as of now. Will get self fired if finds out about setting up trail and instigating spiking of juice.

Solution: Avoid at all costs.

*Prakash*

Problem: Knows that self's friend spiked juice. Has threatened to tell all if self doesn't keep secret of the closet safe. Believes that self knows secret. Self doesn't know secret.

Solution: Mumu to find secret to enable threat back.

*Avinash*

Problem: He exists. (*Then I scratched that out and wrote*) Wants Anuradha on the *Azura* cover but not willing to pay money.

Solution: Get the shoot done. Run away to distant country post shoot. Note to self: find out visa details for Peru.

Then I thought about Mumu and her determination to uncover Prakash's dirty secrets, Tanya sitting under a shamiana and determinedly losing her sanity, my mother's insistence on seeing me married at the next given *shubh mahurat* and the bleak economic climate that made it impossible to find a job less likely to give me ulcers. My head began to ache. This was tougher than I had ever thought possible. I gave myself another good shake and some of my Badass Babe of Boardrooms self-image came back. I could nail this.

I called Mumu and asked her to get me the clothes from Varun's studio. I did not want to see him lest he interpret my walking past his desk as another come-hither move. No problem at all, said Mumu, I will drop by on Tuesday morning and collect them for you.

'Have you changed your mind about Prakash?' I asked.

'Changed my mind? Of course not! I have already started noting down his entry and exit timings from the office. I will do this in my usual meticulous fashion. Wait and watch, you will know in no time what that man is up to,' said Mumu grandly.

'That is what I am afraid of,' I said morosely.

Zoya called to assure me that Rohan Vaidya would indeed be available to discuss the concept of the shoot with me and the people from the magazine on the discussed date.

'Are you sure you'll be the only one coming in from your office?' she asked.

'Yeah, I have it all under control. I'll see you soon,' I said bravely.

'Normally, someone from the advertising agency would accompany you too,' she said, a shadow of doubt evident in her voice.

'Nah! Just me,' I said again. Zoya did not say anymore though the words 'It's your funeral' hung heavy in the air.

I'd had no experience of shoots in my previous job. The client I serviced had had just about enough money to buy a few radio spots and some hoardings. Perhaps I should have stuck about a little longer, I thought wildly to myself, I would have gotten some more exposure to life-changing experiences.

Over the next few nights, my dreams were filled with images of people walking about on tripods instead of legs and blinding flashes going out regularly. It would not be an overstatement to say that I had the shoot on my mind.

Mumu was true to her word and collected the clothes from Varun's studio on Tuesday.

'Here,' she said as she deposited a carton next to my desk. 'The clothes are all here. Take a look. And Varun gives you his best and also says that "you know what *that* means, hint, hint, wink, wink, nudge, nudge".' I looked up at her in horrified silence. To her credit, she looked straight-faced enough. I personally would have infinitely preferred the point-finger-and-laugh approach. Then she gave me a sympathetic pat on the arm and returned to her station outside the Bat's office. I took out the clothes and sifted through them. The moony-eyed chap seemed to have got it all right despite everything. I counted everything off the list that I had prepared. Now I just needed to go for the meeting and make sure the fittings went well.

That evening I decided to call it a day a little early. I went to let Lardie know.

'Shipra,' I said, tentatively, 'I'm off.'

For a volcano, she was giving me remarkably icy treatment. She carried on staring at her computer. What was she finding so interesting there anyway? Must be some gossip website devoted to the life and times of Bollywood actors. I turned to go.

'So, have you got the clothes for the fitting?' she asked, still looking at the computer.

'Yes,' I said, grateful for just being spoken to like a human rather than like a particularly malodorous skunk. 'I'm not supposed to keep them overnight for just a meeting so I've left them here in office. The meeting is at nine in the morning, so I'll come by early, collect them and then head to the venue.'

'I can drop them off at *Azura*,' she offered unexpectedly. 'I'm meeting the advertising agency that side of town anyway.'

I looked at her in silence. What was this, a peace offering? Or was she trying to sabotage my meeting? Was I supposed to meet her halfway? Or was I supposed to agree with gravity and fall for it? The mind spun with all sorts of possibilities. Then in my usual decisive fashion, I said, 'Yeah, sure. Although ... I mean ... well, alright. But drop them by eight forty-five latest?'

'Hmm,' she said in the affable manner that we all knew and loved and went back to her perusal of the computer screen.

On my way out I stopped at Mumu's desk and explained the situation to her.

'I did not want to reject her offer of help, just in case it was genuine, you see,' I said, sounding a trifle confused even to my own ears, 'but I would be foolish to trust her blindly. So tomorrow morning, can you come by a little early, ensure that she is taking the carton of clothes out at the right time and then call me? And if she isn't...'

'I'll get it myself,' said Mumu, proving herself to be the sort of person who makes prosperity more brilliant by sharing and lightens adversity by dividing it. A good, non-rotten egg all around, if you know what I'm saying. Feeling heartened by this display of goodwill, I went home and dined in the company of rotten eggs, which is to say that Urvashi and Menaka were both home early.

# *ten*

I took a taxi to the magazine studio in the morning and messaged Mumu to check if she was up and all was well. All was well, she said; she was on her way to work and would let me know the status upon arrival. I reached *Azura* well before the appointed time and spent it fretting about whether Lardie would actually deliver the clothes. Finally the text from Mumu arrived saying that she had seen Lardie take the carton of clothes with her. I called Mumu.

'Are you sure they were clothes?' I asked. 'She may be bringing me rocks.'

'Yes,' Mumu said patiently. 'Any clothes leaving the building need to have a challan issued from the security guards. I spoke to them, so chill, I know that's what she's got with her.'

I tried to calm down and then went inside the studio to meet Rohan Vaidya and Zoya. Vaishali was there too. I complimented her on her weight loss and then turned my attention to Rohan Vaidya.

He was a tall man. I looked for crazy hair. None. Only salt and pepper tresses. Body art. None. Piercings. None. At least not on any visible body part. He was dressed casually, no big brands, no hippie chic. Nothing at all gave away his celebrity photographer status. I had googled him and found a lot of his work, but it appeared like he guarded his privacy zealously. This was a surprise for me. I was in awe and wanted at once to make a good impression.

'Hi,' I said and extended my hand. 'I am Mini Shukla from JR Enterprises. It's a pleasure to meet you.' He took my hand and smiled warmly and continued to look very cool and collected. I felt like I was just a stand-in for my parents while they were away, so grown-up did he appear. Perhaps it was this discomfiture that made me proceed to put my foot in my mouth.

'You are older than I imagined,' I said, sending waves of shock carousing through the room. 'Uh, I don't mean that you're *old*. What I mean is that you just *look* older.' Vaishali and Zoya gawped at me.

Rohan saved the day.

'I don't know which one is the greater evil, really. To your credit, I think you're younger than I had imagined. Perhaps a case of overachievement?' he twinkled at me. I felt my cheeks warming.

'Err, yes, actually my boss was supposed to come too for this meeting but now it will be just me,' I said, wishing that anyone other than me was handling this stupid, stupid shoot.

'Well, that's good. We have you all to ourselves. Now, let's discuss some concepts. Vaishali? Zoya?' he said and opened a notebook.

'Parrots!' said Vaishali, looking very pleased with herself.

'Parrots with their greens and reds! Amazing! And sheep! Soft, luxuriant, feminine.' Zoya nodded encouragingly.

She couldn't be serious. What was this, a shoot at the zoo?

Rohan did not say much, just wrote in his notebook. A peon entered the room with a carton to say that the clothes had been delivered for me. I thanked my stars as Vaishali continued to talk of parrots and their feathers and sheep and their wool. A model-like girl, all arms and legs and an impossibly flat abdomen walked in and took a seat in the corner and started to read a magazine.

'Cockatoos, I am thinking, RV, with all the tropical burst of colour. Have you noticed how the fall-winter colours are all about parrots this time? And the sheep providing a certain warmth? What do you think?'

'They're meant to,' he said wryly and then turned to me. 'What do you think, Mini? It's your brand. Is there any obvious conflict between this concept and the brand's values?'

I tried to think, but my brain seemed to have trouble receiving oxygen. I looked at him nervously and forced myself to recount the brand's values. Some parts of the presentation I had made to Vaishali came back to me. 'Well yes, except that animal rights groups might object to our using parrots and sheep for the shoot,' I said.

Vaishali frowned at this. Her parrots seemed to be taking wings.

'Art is not about these practical matters,' she said.

'I like your concept, Vee,' Rohan said soothingly, 'but Mini is right. And there may be some practical difficulties in controlling the animals. How about we use feathers instead?

Thousands of them? All faux, but will look real. You can have all the colour you want!'

Vaishali simmered down.

'Yes, I guess we could do that, though some parrots and some sheep should be there,' she said with a pout. Zoya nodded some more.

'Well, we can see about that, can't we? The cover is being paid for by JRE, so I guess we cannot get too wild with the concept, eh? Let's just stick to what the brand needs,' said Rohan.

I couldn't help warming to him. He was looking after me, like a well-meaning uncle.

Some more discussion followed. I did not have too much to contribute, not knowing the first thing about such shoots. Vaishali was quite the veteran, delving into the condition of light and the exact camera angles. Rohan humoured her while sticking to his own. Zoya occasionally rolled her eyes when she caught my glance. I felt like a little girl in the company of occasionally indulgent adults. Rohan asked questions of me and answered them himself, making me out to be quite the expert on all matters of cover-shoots. For that I felt like throwing my arms around him and giving a whooping cheer.

Finally he turned to the model who had all but turned invisible.

'Suki, let's try a few looks, shall we?' Suki got up obediently and came forward to take the clothes from me.

'We'll have the stylist and your designer with us at the shoot, of course. For now, I just want to get a good look at what we have here,' Rohan said as I looked on with what I hoped was an intelligent expression. 'We'll be able to tell if the clothes fit with the concept we have in mind.'

I handed over the first of the combinations that I had prepared to the model. She went inside the changing room and took forever changing into them.

'So, Mini,' said Rohan to me in a kind voice as we waited for the model to emerge, 'how long have you been with JRE?'

I furiously contemplated inflating my work experience with the company to a decade or more and then quickly realised the futility of the exercise.

'Just under a year,' I said, a trifle more quietly than I had intended to. He smiled at me again. 'But this is not my first job,' I hastily clarified, lest he take me for a complete rookie.

'That's good. Planning to last a while longer?' he asked genially, and I would have answered in a supremely confident affirmative except for Suki the model who emerged from the dressing room at that point.

'This is not happening,' she giggled.

Oh dear lord. The clothes hung from her tiny frame looking just about as flattering as a stray kite caught on an electricity pole and fluttering about aimlessly. To say that they were loose would be like saying Mount Everest is a pretty spiffy hill. The top threatened to fall down from her skinny shoulders. She was holding the trousers up with her hands.

'Unless you are going for the kaftan look?' she said. Zoya burst out laughing and hastily stifled her mirth.

'What's going on here?' said Vaishali and walked up to the model. 'What size are these clothes?'

'I had picked a size medium,' I said stupidly. Rohan stood there silently, watching the spectacle unfold, a spectacle that I had created with my own hands.

Vaishali reached over and checked the label. She then looked at me coldly. 'These are size XXL!' she said.

Bloody Lardie! She had got me and got me in a way that I was least expecting. She sent me the clothes alright, just managed to switch them all for three sizes bigger. My cheeks were burning up. All eyes were on me.

'I ... I ...  I'm sorry. I think there was some mistake,' I faltered and searched around wildly for words, any words that could me look like a little less of a moron. Zoya came bravely to my defence.

'Maybe you can call your workplace and ask them to send us smaller sizes?' she said. Vaishali silenced her with a look that could have made fresh magma grow icicles.

'I'm sorry. I can't waste any more time waiting for the clothes to arrive. I have a meeting with the advertising guys in twenty minutes. Zoya, please sort this out,' she said, and with an air-kiss to Rohan, marched out of the office. She would talk to Lardie about the moron that was her flunky and both of them would cackle about the incredible foolishness  of some juniors. Zoya made assenting sounds and turned to me.

'Maybe you should call for the right clothes, Mini,' she said. Before I could say anything, Suki spoke up.

'I'm sorry, ya, but I need to get going too. I have another audition for an item number at a studio in Andheri. I will need to start for there soon. I was told this would be a quick job,' she said, looking like a couple dozen curtains were billowing merrily about her. I tried to think of something to hold her back, something to set this mess straight. I didn't even dare look at Rohan. Just when I had wanted to establish myself as a seasoned, hard-nosed corporate woman, there I was — coming across as an A-grade doofus.

'Well, alright then. I think we might as well call this meeting off,' said Rohan as I turned a darker shade of crimson. 'Zoya, nice to meet you. Let me know what the next step is.'

'I will,' said Zoya as she took his hand. Suki went back to change into clothes more befitting her size.

'What happened there?' asked Zoya when we were alone.

'My boss happened!' I said, sitting down heavily and burying my head in my hands. 'It's a long story, the gist being that my boss hates me and would much rather see me burnt at the stake than turn up for work, if you know what I mean.'

Zoya raised her eyebrows. 'Well, whatever it is, you ruined this meeting, Mini,' she stated bluntly causing me to groan loudly. Suki came out, returned the clothes to me and with air-kisses all around left for her audition. I started putting the clothes back in their carton, marvelling at how much bigger they looked once it was established that they were actually made for the Loch Ness monster.

'Can't you complain to her boss?' Zoya asked, a little more kindly.

'Only if I like being stung by poisonous insects,' I said, wishing someone would lock Lardie in a haunted castle with hundreds of bored ghosts hounding her, woo, woo, woo.

'Hmm,' said Zoya contemplatively. 'Well, you need help obviously. Listen, I will reschedule this meeting. Get the right clothes and guard them with your life. I will speak to Rohan and Vaishali. I don't think you'll really need to be there. I will handle everything and then tell you how it goes. Alright?'

I nodded miserably. People were asking me to stay away from meetings now, for fear of untold misfortune descending upon them. What was next? A promotion did not seem to be the correct answer for some reason. Zoya left the room with a pat on my back, probably meaning to communicate solidarity but managing to convey pity instead.

I packed the clothes and trudged back to office. Mumu saw me as I passed by her desk.

'All well?' she asked and then whispered, 'I think I am on to something.'

I nodded absently and continued walking to my desk. The mind and the heart were all aflutter with confusion, the sort that Christopher Columbus might have felt when he was told that what he had discovered after months of sailing the seas was not Asia as he had believed all along but America instead. Quite shaken, if you get my meaning.

I saw Lardie sitting at her desk. She looked up as she saw me. It would be fair to say that the bitter fire of malice burnt deep in her eyes. I walked up to her. Women of lesser experience would have expected Lardie to be contrite. I did not.

'You changed the clothes for larger ones,' I said flatly.

She widened her eyes at me.

'You sound upset,' she said.

'Upset?' I said, attempting some slow and deep breathing that might have succeeded in calming down sages from bygone eras but was proving to be painfully inadequate in a modern-day office setting. 'I would say I am furious but that would be untrue. The fact is, I should have expected this from you and now I am burning with rage at my decision to trust someone who has proved herself to be quite the snake in the past.'

She put down her pen and leaned back in her chair.

'Oh dear,' she said. 'This is just some character building that I thought would serve you well. I do hope Rohan Vaidya and Vee were not too upset with the whole mix-up.'

I tried to kill her with a look, failed and then turned to go back to my seat.

'Just a reminder that you need to refuse any purple flowers that head your way,' she said, not looking at me.

'Not if they mark your funeral,' I muttered darkly under my breath and sat down to mull over my latest misfortunes. The carton with the right-sized clothes lay hidden under my table. Lardie had been very careful in carrying out her evil plan.

I went out to smoke a quick cigarette and discovered that Mumu was there too, pretending to smoke out of a thin pipe. It looked elegant and remarkably fake. I stood in a shaded corner, hoping that she would not see me, leaving me to stew alone in my misery. As always, that was too much to hope for. She bounded over as soon as she caught sight of me.

'I have observed Prakash's actions over the last few days

and I have concluded that he disappears for hours on end whenever Avinash is not around,' she said, mysterious as always.

'Is that so?' I said absently, still burning up at the memory of my blunder at *Azura*.

'And I trailed him a few times and he always seems to head for the basement,' continued Mumu. 'So unless he is helping Tanya plan her wedding trousseau, he goes into the supply closet.'

'Well, I am fairly certain that he is browsing all sorts of pornographic sites; it's against the rules of course, but in this madhouse one can never say what people will get away with.'

'No Mini,' said Mumu with something like conviction in her voice. 'It's not that. He is really jittery that we have stumbled upon his secret. It's serious.'

'Well, you are on the case, detective,' I said and stubbed out a pensive cigarette with a doleful foot. 'So we need not worry, right?'

Mumu puffed up with pride at this declaration of confidence in her abilities. She walked away after this, possibly to eavesdrop on conversations.

The phone rang soon after I was back at my desk.

'Hello,' I said mournfully.

'Did your meeting go well?' asked a voice at the other end. I groaned inside.

'Hello Varun,' I said carefully. 'Yes, everything's okay. Thanks for the clothes. I might need them again soon, so I'll return them to you in a few days.'

'That's okay,' he said and then, 'How about a cup of coffee then? We can go to the bistro after work.'

Hmm, his girlfriend must be out of town, I thought. I looked nervously in Lardie's direction. She would probably mix my blood in the coffee and then drink it if she caught me with Varun.

'Erm, I'm working till late today. Maybe some other time?' I said.

'Alright,' he sounded disappointed. I wondered at the capriciousness of the human female as I hung up. This was the same man who made the flowers in the garden of my heart bloom at one point and now he couldn't even make a weed grow. Then I thought about his girlfriend and decided that the human male was pretty capricious too.

What a day this was turning out to be, I thought as I ordered a cup of tea to soothe my nerves. Then I decided to take something for the headache that had taken home in my temples. I took out a Dispirin and walked to the water cooler to get some water.

'A headache, dear?' I heard from behind me. Even without turning around, I could sense the slime ooze all over the floor.

'What is it, Prakash?' I asked without turning around.

'Ask that Mumtaaz to lay off,' he said, his voice hardening, forcing me to look at him.

'What do you mean?' I tried to look blank as I groaned inside. That Mumu might as well wave a large, red banner when she went following people.

'I know she is trying to keep a check on me,' said Prakash.

'I know you people are after evidence. Be careful, or you and your friends might get hurt.'

'You are just paranoid. We all have work to do and no one is following you,' I said and tried to brush past him.

'I suggest you keep to the work then. I have been around much longer, Mini, and I will tie you up in knots that you won't be able to untangle for years,' said Prakash and walked off. Well, the least a man could do after he has extended a hearty threat was let a girl have the last word. That Prakash was really rude.

And dangerous. I went to tell Mumu that she had been unable to be quite as invisible as she had imagined and to stop her pursuit of Prakash. As expected, Mumu refused to listen to me.

Zoya called me the next day.

'Hey, I have managed to reschedule the fittings. Just get me the clothes next Thursday and I will organise everything,' she said.

'Thank you so much, Zoya, I can't tell you how much I appreciate this,' I said, my heart bursting with gratitude.

'It's okay, Mini. Your company is paying for this cover so we need to work on this together. Just don't mess up again, okay?' she said.

'I won't,' I said. 'Uh, how about the photographer? Was he furious about how things turned out?' My face turned crimson at a picture of the famous man laughing about my faux pas over drinks with his buddies, all of them seasoned men of the world, not bumbling idiots who struggled to get a simple dress-size right.

'Naah, not really. So next step, we will just discuss the look that we want for the shoot. Please e-mail your requirements to me and I will make sure they get covered,' she said.

I promised to do so and went back to my work. Lardie was really piling it up for me, possibly petrified that if accorded a single spare moment, I might use it to fix a secret rendezvous with Varun. Technically it was impossible for Lardie to be more overbearing, but she was nothing if not an overachiever. I mulled a little over the Lardie problem. She needed to know that I was not interested in responding to Varun's advances.

How?

I could send her an anonymous note! A note saying that Varun had a girlfriend stashed away and that I was not the one she needed to fear. Then I put myself in Lardie's oversized shoes and came to the conclusion that the first person she would point to with all her twenty stubby fingers and toes would be me. No, this would not work. I would just have to duck into dark corners to avoid Varun at all costs.

I delivered the clothes to Zoya personally on the appointed day. She told me that Rohan was running a little late but Suki the model was already in and ready to change.

'Vaishali still wants her parrots, though she has given up on the sheep,' she told me. 'What do you think?'

I thought about it. 'Let it be. I don't want her to start having second thoughts about Anuradha again,' I said. 'I guess we will just need to make sure that the birds don't go about messing the clothes. No droppings and all, if you know what I mean.'

'We have handled other crazy covers in the past, don't

worry. You should leave, the others will be in soon,' she said and went off in search of Suki. I walked towards the exit, my ego reduced to the size of a raisin left out in the sun for too long, and almost did not see Rohan Vaidya as he came in.

'Ah, the young achiever from JR Enterprises,' he said. I looked up.

'Uh … uh, yes, hello. I was just leaving,' I said.

'What? Left the clothes back at the office again?' he asked, grinning.

'No! I just came by to drop the clothes off,' I said uncomfortably. 'You guys decide on the concept and I will see you at the shoot.'

'Why? Shouldn't you be a part of this meeting?' he asked. I didn't know how to answer that without making a complete ass of myself so I stayed silent.

'Oh! Let me see, is this because of Vee's little tantrum that day?' he asked. I continued to add to the conversation with my silence. This was not good. I could not agree without appearing to criticise Vaishali. Consequently, though, this meant that the eminent Mr Vaidya would think of me not just as an oaf, but an inarticulate oaf at that.

'Oh come on, Mini, let's go inside,' he said and took my hand, leading the way to the large fitting room. 'We will see to it that Vee doesn't terrorise you too much.'

'It's not her fault,' I dragged my feet as I was swept across the corridor, trying to halt the progress of the determined man with me. 'I really messed up. I wasted everyone's time. I shouldn't be here!' I finally managed to stop. He looked at me in exasperation.

'Mini,' he said calmly, 'anyone in their right mind could see that something underhanded had been done to your clothes that day. You looked positively shaken, a tad blanched even, like a tomato left in hot water.'

'You saw that?' I asked, hope suddenly bursting forth in my heart. 'Did you really?'

He nodded. I decided to take him into confidence.

'Between you and me, I don't think Vaishali could strictly qualify as a person in her right mind. Plus, she was so angry when the clothes fiasco took place and I really need her on my side right now. I … well, I don't have too much going for me at work.'

He stared at me.

'Well then, come for this meeting and prove that you are not a nitwit,' he said confidently. 'Why are you hiding this way?'

'The thing is — I'm not sure that I'm *not* a nitwit,' I said sadly. 'Everything seems to be topsy-turvy right now.'

'Alright, maybe that's true. But trust me, it will become turvy-topsy if you just give it your best for long enough,' he said, propelling me into the room. Vaishali was there with Suki and Zoya. Vaishali's eyes narrowed when she saw me. Zoya threw me a look of disbelief. I stared at the ground and threw it a plea to swallow me whole and spare me their disapproving glances. Only Suki continued to look around vacantly, oblivious to the tension. She was wearing an Angel outfit and it looked great on her, even to my fashion-inexperienced eyes.

'Hello all,' said Rohan, keeping his bags in the corner with one hand and pushing me further inside with the other. 'We are in luck. Mini will be able to join us after all. Vee, my love, how do you manage to look so gorgeous? Suki, she will run you out of business, eh, tall order though that is. Zoya, nice shoes!' He charmed all three women with one fell swoop and pushed me into a chair. Vaishali thawed under his attention, and with Rohan's encouragement I started to make a few (excellent, I thought) points about the concept. It felt good to be able to contribute something other than just staying the hell out of everyone's faces, and when the meeting ended an hour later, it could be said with reasonable accuracy that I was deeply grateful to Rohan for pushing me into the meeting. Maybe the world was not only about Lardies and Bats and Oilmen. It was about good-hearted photographers too.

'Thanks,' I said, as we walked out of the *Azura* office.

'No problem,' he answered, taking out a cigarette and lighting it. I stared at it hungrily. He caught my look and offered me one. I took it and inhaled deeply when he lit it for me. We stood under a tree, impossible as it sounds in Mumbai, and smoked quietly.

'Once upon a time, we could have had coffee with this,' he reminisced sadly, possibly thinking about the days when cafés still allowed smoking within their premises.

'Yes, though I must admit, I've cut down heavily since the ban,' I said. 'So maybe there is some good in bad after all.'

'And that is what you need to think when things go from bad to awful at work,' he said.

'You don't know my boss,' I sighed. 'And you don't want to either.'

'You have to be smart, Mini,' he said, stubbing out his cigarette with his shoe and then picking it up and placing in his bag. 'Learn the rules and play by them. Expect the worst from everyone at all times.'

'Yes, I guess,' I said. 'Though what sort of a person would that make me? I mean, not everyone is an ogre. I do have a Tanya and a Prithvi and they can and almost always are complete morons, but they don't wish me dead.'

Rohan laughed.

'You're quite a child still,' he said. 'Come on, it's time to get that coffee.'

He deftly bundled me into his car and we were sitting at a café before I could say 'cheese sandwich'. He took pictures of me as I mulled over the hundred and twenty varieties in the menu before declaring that it was all just coffee. At first, I felt like a bug, living its little life under a scientist's gaze, but soon I realised that the camera had become an extra limb that I would have to ignore.

'Or a giant wart on the tip of your nose,' I told him. 'Or a proboscis that you were born with. Unfortunate, but there all the same.'

'Your teeth are crooked,' he said from behind the camera. 'Funny how I never notice these things unless I see them through a lens.'

I stopped smiling and pursed my lips tight over my crooked teeth.

'Oh don't bother,' he said. 'It won't help. I think it lends you an edge.'

'Just because you hang out with supermodels doesn't mean you should insult poor, ugly working girls,' I whined and then looked at my watch.

'I need to go,' I said. 'This has been nice but Lardie feels lovesick if I'm not around.'

Rohan said he would pay for my coffee. He planned to hang about a little longer.

'Thanks,' I said. 'I would have insisted on paying, but my mother says it's an elder's privilege.'

I could hear him guffawing as I walked out of the café and into the sunshine.

# eleven

Three days before the shoot, I was running through several mental and actual checklists. There were post-its everywhere on my workstation bearing things-to-do lists. I could not leave anything to that unpredictable thing called chance. I would be a corporate highflier if that was the last thing I did. Then I thought of Avinash and his refusal to pay Anuradha's fees and I decided that in all likelihood this shoot would be the last thing I did. Sooner or later, one of the two would definitely decide that I was the root of all evil and a piercing in the heart with a sacred trishul was what I deserved. Then, as it happens with such things, they would secure my mortal remains in a coffin and mark it with a cross. There I would remain for hundreds of years till a young couple decided to spend a rainy night in the ghostly, lonely mansion that would be my haunt. I thought about how I could not give up on bad punning even in the afterlife.

I forced myself to push macabre thoughts out of my mind and went through yet another list, one of the points of which was:

• Remind Rohan about the shoot

This was one of my few pleasurable tasks. In the last few weeks, Rohan had called me quite a few times and he had always been nothing short of completely charming, causing me to not give up on the human race in its entirety. I mailed him.

*Rohan* (I wrote),

*I know I have not spoken of anything else these last few days, but land up at the shoot.*

*Mini*

Then I looked at the next item on the list.

- Get clothes from Varun. P.S. Wear invisibility cloak while doing so; should not be seen with Varun.

Hmm, this would be difficult. I decided to enlist Mumu's help. I dialled her extension.

'I need your help again,' I said. 'You need to get some clothes for my shoot from Varun. I'm trying to avoid him.'

'I don't want to leave my seat for too long,' she said. 'I'm watching Prakash, as you are well aware.'

'Oh yes, I almost forgot that you are still on that case. If he decides to do away with you and your investigation one of these days, let me know what you want on your epitaph.'

Mumu grunted at this and told me that she would get the clothes I needed from Varun. Since the threat that Prakash had good-naturedly extended, she had given up on following him around, but she still watched him carefully, hoping that sooner or later he would drop a clue about his secret.

I moved to the next item in the list.

- Confirm shoot with Anuradha

I dialled Anuradha's phone. There was no response. I sent

her a text message and moved on to the next thing that I needed to do.

• Sanity check on Tanya

I sighed at this one. Tanya had made serious progress in her wedding planning, but in the process she had become the most-feared creature of them all — a bridezilla. Unchecked by any boss, unfettered by the demands of work, this monster had grown and now she needed to drink a supplier's blood first thing in the morning before she could see the world clearly. Prithvi had begged me to take out time to visit her in her lair in the basement every day and ensure that there were no hidden bodies rotting away under her desk. It needed to be done. I called Tanya.

'Hey Tan,' I forced myself to sound cheerful, nervous that the wrong tone could set off an attack. 'Just thought I'd say hello before I get back to my all-consuming shoot.'

'Hang on!' she barked and then, 'Listen to this.'

Suddenly, instead of Tanya's voice, loud music started blaring in my ears.

'*When a man loves a woman,*' Michael Bolton crooned, '*he will run to the edge of the world....*'

'What do you think?' Tanya asked me faintly from the background.

'Err, nice,' I said, uncertainly.

'Yeah but the question is — is it nice enough to be played at the reception? Now listen to this!' she changed something on her CD player and the Beatles came on with *I want to hold your hand.*

'This is good too.' Prithvi had told me that nothing could

be anything but nice when Tanya asked for one's opinion these days, and I was inclined to agree with him.

'Yeah, but is it good enough?' she repeated. Then she warmed up to the theme. 'Do you have any idea just how many songs there are in this world? Do you? Thousands! Millions! Trillions! And different genres. Rock, instrumental, rhythm and blues, soul, country, classical. Western classical, Indian classical. Within Indian classical, there's Hindustani and Carnatic … what am I supposed to do, huh? You think it's easy, you call everything nice, what about me? Does anyone think about me? Bloody music industry is out to get me.'

Oh dear, this was going to be tougher than I thought. I tried to get a word in.

'May I ask something? Why are you even looking at classical music? In all the years that I have known you, I have never once heard either you or Prithvi listen to classical music.'

'So?' she asked suspiciously. 'What is your point?'

'My point is this—' I braced myself for a tantrum and continued, '—shouldn't the music that you play at your wedding mean something to you?'

All was silent for a few seconds.

'You mean it doesn't need to be perfect,' she finally said thoughtfully. 'Just meaningful?'

'Um, I guess it will be perfect if it's meaningful,' I said and thought to myself, *Here it comes, the raging tornado spurred on by bridal fury.*

She didn't say anything immediately.

'Tanya?' I finally asked, trepidation dripping from every word. 'What is it? Are you alright? Look, you can have any music you want, don't be upset.'

In reply, she started sobbing loudly.

'You!' she bawled. 'You are my best friend!'

Oh, so these were not tears of frustration at my limited understanding of all things bridal.

'Um yes, I guess I am,' I agreed tentatively, not very sure about how to play this on the front foot.

'You show me the true path every time,' she wailed. 'You are an angel sent to guide me.'

'That's good, right?' I asked.

'It is, it is! In fact, I have decided, you will perform the main song at my *sangeet*. You deserve it! Just get a partner though. Now I need to fish out the first mixed tape that Pri gave me. Or was it a CD? We will play that. I love you! Bye!' she hung up on me.

Augh! A dance? Worse, dance with a partner? I decided to bail out of this unforeseen pleasure by seeking higher counsel.

'Hello Pri,' I said as soon as he answered his phone. 'Your wife-to-be is slowly heading for a padded cell.'

'Yes, I know,' he said sympathetically, 'and to think I will have to share the cell with her.'

'Listen, she wants me to do a dance routine with a partner at the *sangeet*. I obviously can't.' I came to the point, not wanting to beat about the bush, not having anything against bushes.

'Why not?' he demanded.

'Well, other than my two left feet, there is the problem of not having the two right feet of a partner,' I explained patiently.

'I see. Well, what can I say? These days when Tanya asks you to do something, you bow down from the waist or do a curtsey as the case may be and just shut up and do it.'

'What? Why, you hen-pecked little…' I started.

'Don't waste your breath, Mini,' he interrupted. 'I am thick-skinned for a reason. It helps the water slide off. Now I need to go — am in a bit of a spot at work.'

'Why, what happened?' I asked grumpily.

'My boss went to London for a vacation. This morning she told us that every time she says "Mama went to London", her two-year-old daughter starts singing "London Bridge is falling down". I couldn't resist asking her if the child knew that she was talking about cause and effect. The boss is pretty sore since then and I am massaging her feet and ego alternately. Take care.'

I hung up. Of all the women in the world, I had to be friends with the most masterful of them all. Anyway, it was time to get back to my to-do list. I decided to call Anuradha again. This time she answered.

'Hello Mini,' she said. 'I just saw that you called a while back too. I was sleeping. Late night shoot again. I'm in Kerala.'

'Oh alright,' I said. 'So when are you back? Tomorrow or day after?'

'Oh I am here for the next week,' she said and I heard her sip something. The earth stopped rotating on its axis. For a moment my heart stopped beating and then it started making up for lost time by pounding for all that it was worth. Questions were whirring about my mind like a lost fan.

What was this air-head talking about? She needed to be here, in Mumbai, getting shot … shooted … photographed in any case, by the famous Rohan Vaidya wearing the trendy but eminently affordable Angel clothes.

'What are you talking about, Anuradha? How can you be there for a week? You need to be here in Mumbai this Friday — for my shoot,' my breath was getting stuck in my throat. This was a disaster the proportions of which I could not even begin to contemplate.

'Oh? Well, you never confirmed that you needed me there on the date we had decided earlier. So I just went ahead and took up this assignment. Sorry sweets, maybe next time?' she said airily.

Next time? There would be no next time. I thought of my struggles with Vaishali to get Anuradha on the cover, the mishap with the clothes at the fitting and the endless coordination that I'd done for this shoot. Hours and hours of work, millions of phone-calls, calling in favours, getting treated like dirt by everyone including the office-boys, just so this beautiful creature could get a cover to her name. And here she was, telling me that she would do it the next time? *Next time?* I would show her next time.

'I did confirm, Anuradha,' I said as coldly as I could, considering hot lava was flowing out of my ears at this point. 'Check your mail, won't you? I'd like you to refer to my mail dated…'

'Oh shit, you did, did you? Looks like I messed up then, huh,' she said before I could complete my sentence. 'But this assignment is also really prestigious, you know, and I cannot just ask them to bugger off mid-way.'

The hot magma was now forming little puddles around my feet, steam emanating from its hot self.

'I see. It appears to me that you don't think a cover shoot is very prestigious,' I said, with what could be called a definite trace of sarcasm.

'It's not that, ya! Look, for one thing, everyone knows that this cover is paid-for. Second, I am not a brand ambassador for you guys, just a one-time model. And third, it's not like I have been paid in advance. Things keep changing in this industry. Why don't you get someone else? I can give you Geetanjali's number...' she said, oblivious to the fact that her little mess-up with her black book could cost me my job, hell, would *definitely* cost me my job.

There were only two options to handle this problem. I could take premature *sanyaas* and call it a day as far as a career was concerned, wistfully sighing when someone asked me about what happened to my job, throwing up my hands as I did it, picking up *'sab kismet ka khel hai'* or *'yeh sab moh-maaya hai'* as my chosen explanation.

Or I could tell this harebrained idiot where to get off.

'Listen to me, Anuradha,' I said. 'My job depends on this shoot going well. If you don't turn up, I will lose my job. If I lose my job, I will turn into a manic person with loads of free time on her hands. If I have all this free time, I will use it to plan only one thing and that would be revenge on the one person who caused me all this trouble. So I think now is the time you make your choice about which way you want to roll this particular ball.' I stopped for breath.

There was an audible gulp from the other side.

'Come on, Mini, there's no need to sound like that. It is just a shoot, for chrissake...'

'Get your ass on the next plane to Mumbai or I will personally come and catch you by your tail and drag you all the way back,' I shouted, losing the last vestige of patience with her.

'Hey, you cannot speak to me like this,' she said, sounding most affronted.

'Oh yeah? Well, get this my lovely, by the time I finish this phone call, if I do not have your assurance that you are coming right back to Mumbai and doing my shoot, I will call up each and every corporate house and advertising agency in this country and inform them of your incompetence and unprofessional attitude. Believe me, I will have plenty of time to do it, you moron,' I screamed, my face an unbecoming shade of crimson with anger and despair.

Anuradha was understandably taken aback by this sudden display of insanity.

'I must say you are being really tough on me, Mini. I never thought of you as difficult. Whatever! I will call you back later,' she said and hung up.

I put down the phone and tried to breathe deeply. Then I put my hands on my cheeks to cool them down. Well, this was it. I had really gone and done it now. I had lost my temper at one of the leading models of our times. Avinash would hear of this and he would lose no time in asking me to collect my final dues the next time I was passing by the area. The more I thought about it, the more prepared I got to pack my meagre belongings in a small carton and say my goodbyes to my few well-wishers. The shoot on which my life had hung had not even happened and already I was on my way to being booted out. Maybe Bat and Lardie had been right all along, maybe I *was* a worthless piece of inefficiency. It was a decidedly deflated Mini Shukla that picked up her phone to talk to currently deranged best friend about her cup of woe that was currently overflowing when the phone rang.

Anuradha! I gulped and pressed the green button that connected me to the lovely lady at the other end.

'Mini,' she began. I braced myself for what was coming.

'Yes, Anuradha,' I said humbly.

'I have managed to speak to the coordinator here and she will finish my part by tomorrow morning somehow and I will come down to Mumbai by tomorrow evening. Is that alright?' she said.

Huh?

'Ye...es,' I managed to get out.

'Listen, I'm sorry for putting you in a tight spot. I really messed up my calendar,' she said. In that moment I knew without a doubt that she had taken up the Kerala assignment on purpose. There was no mistake; she had tried to see if she could get away with it, and my meltdown had communicated in no uncertain terms that she, in fact, could not mess around with the hot-blooded Shukla clan.

'Yeah, that's cool. Just turn up for the shoot, yes?' I said.

'I'll be there,' she said and hung up again.

I gave a war-whoop and threw some A4 sheets into the air.

'Who da man?' I asked myself.

'Me!' I answered. Technically incorrect, but why not, in the spirit of the moment.

'Who da best?' I asked yet another pertinent question.

'Me!' I replied and got up to do a little jig.

Mumu came by to catch me doing pelvic thrusts and raised an eyebrow.

'What happened, Mini?' she asked quietly.

'Corporate bitches are made, not born,' I announced my fresh learning to the world.

'Oh. I wanted to tell you that I think I know how to get Prakash,' she said in a composed manner.

'Really? How?' I asked, curious in spite of myself. Inside, the bubble of happiness was still intact. I was a bully, I could call people's bluffs and make them do my bidding. There was nothing to fear anymore.

'We need to catch him in the act, Mini,' said Mumu in a conspiratorial voice.

'That's not such a brilliant idea,' I said, now suddenly worried that Mumu would meet an untimely end at the hands of Prakash. 'He is dangerous, you know.'

'Maybe, but that's the only way he will ever be caught,' she said.

'Alright,' I said, holding out my hands. 'We will plan out a strategy once my shoot is done. Right now, I am channelling all my energy in just one direction.'

She looked doubtful but nodded anyway.

'I take it you have resolved the payment crisis,' she said, sitting at the edge of my table. 'Going by your little jig there,

I mean, though I suppose it was more of a tribal war dance to celebrate the beheading of the tyrannical dictator.'

That took care of the said bubble of happiness. One moment it was floating about merrily, roughly in the centre of my soul, the second it had made a quiet 'pop' sound and disappeared. I sat down, deflated.

'No,' I said flatly. 'I had almost forgotten about that aspect of my misery. Thanks for reminding me.'

'Well, what do you have in mind? What will you tell Anuradha after she has finished shooting and strolls over to collect her cheque?' Mumu asked another pertinent and timely question.

'I was thinking along the lines of fleeing the country,' I said as I moodily peeled a post-it off the wall. 'But tell me, Mumu, you are Avinash's secretary, is there any way I can get him to change his mind?'

'No,' she said. I waited for her to elaborate but it looked like she was done. I felt more miserable than ever before, not that I could have believed it possible a moment ago.

'Well, there must be something I can do to make him pay up,' I said, banging one fist into a hand, in the universally acknowledged manner of a Hindi film hero declaring frustration and consequently war on the universe.

Mumu considered my passion for the subject and appeared to think deeply for a moment.

'Naah,' she said.

Then she thought some more.

'You could pray,' she said. I shoved her off the desk and asked her to go and track down Prakash or volunteer time for the international symposium of amateur (and I mean, really, *really* amateur) spies or invest herself in any activity that kept her depressing self out of my hair.

The next couple of days passed by in a flurry of activity. Zoya wanted to me check out some parrots that were auditioning for the cover shoot. This was a very stimulating activity. One of the parrots could say cusswords in three different languages. I wanted to give him the part. Zoya demurred.

The day of the shoot dawned bright and clear. I called Anuradha and she confirmed that she would be reporting to the shoot on time. Zoya and Rohan were already at the studio when I walked in with the clothes, as were many other people that I had never seen before.

White screens lined one part of the large hall against which Anuradha would probably stand for the shoot. The marked area was surrounded by different types of lights and reflectors. Some portable fans stood on the floor, which was covered with what looked like a black plastic sheet to me. Most of the people wore black t-shirts and blue jeans and looked really busy. I hung about for a minute, wishing that I had carried a clipboard along. I had read somewhere that a person with a clipboard was always taken seriously.

Finally, Rohan caught sight of me.

'Mini, give the clothes to Neha here,' he pointed at a girl who rushed to take the clothes from me. 'Get them ironed pronto, Neha.' She hurried off to do his bidding.

'Wow, so home turf, huh?' I sidled up to Rohan.

'Um, um,' he said, sounding really professional. Goodness, but how many cameras did he have? I decided to stay out of his hair and make myself useful by just sharing my aura with everyone. Silently.

I wandered over to the make-up room where Anuradha was getting ready. A make-up artist was working on her face, dabbing some lotion on her cheeks like I buttered my toast — liberally. The *Azura* stylist was there too, possibly to add value to the make-up. This was the first time I was seeing Anuradha in person. She was leaning back in her chair and had her eyes closed. Unfinished as she was, it was still quite clear that she commanded the price that she did for a reason. From people who could pay, that is. I decided to postpone showing Anuradha who the real Mini Shukla was and started to look through the array of bottles that lay on the counter.

'You!' said the make-up artist's assistant, a very hip looking girl with mismatched shoes on her feet. 'What do you want? Who are you anyway?'

I gave her one of my special, winning smiles.

'Hey, I'm just looking around. I am from JR Enterprises. Mini Shukla is my name,' I said.

Anuradha opened her eyes at this.

'You!' What? Would everyone refer to me in this rude fashion? 'Really? You are Mini Shukla? I thought you would be one hell of an old hag! You are a child!' Anuradha said and dissolved into giggles. Well, this was most disheartening. I shook her hand as she extended it.

'I am just youthful looking,' I said, trying to sound mature, but Anuradha was evidently in a place where everything sounded very funny. Maybe she was nervous? Zoya came bustling into the room, carrying a tape recorder.

'Hello all,' she said. 'Anuradha, can we start the interview please?'

'Sure, go ahead,' she said, and Zoya started asking her questions.

'How does it feel to be shooting for the *Azura* cover?' started Zoya. Anuradha could answer that in only one way, I supposed.

I wandered out again and wiped my brow. I kept pushing the thought of Anuradha's payment away and it kept bouncing back. I was having mini panic attacks every five minutes. Maybe I could tell her that the cheque was stuck in the system. It was, in a way, and I would not be strictly lying. I could tell her that I would get it out as soon as I could. That would also be true.

Maybe I could ask her to treat this as charity. The 'Save Mini Shukla's Ass Fund'? Then I dismissed that idea. Anuradha would not be inclined to be very kind to me after the way I had hauled her back from a decidedly well-paid assignment in God's own country for what she would soon discover was a pro-bono project.

I spent the next hour worrying about what was to become of me. Anuradha got dressed and came out. The clothes looked fantastic, but then, on that frame, even my old chatai, the one on which my cat slept back home, would look lovely. The parrots were brought out by their keeper, an old lady who ran a pet shelter, who showed Anuradha how to handle them. Anuradha held one of them gingerly. They fluttered under her inexperienced hands and I held my breath thinking that they would settle on this as a good moment for a relaxing bowel movement.

'Beautiful shot,' shouted Rohan and clicked away. Anuradha posed with what is called practised ease. In between shots, Anuradha sat down with Zoya for the interview. I kept reminding her of how she needed to plug the brand. There was a small break for lunch where everyone had coffee and sandwiches. Anuradha had three pieces of popcorn.

All too soon it was done.

'We'll send you the CD so you can select the final image,' Rohan said as he and his team started to pack up.

The moment I had dreaded was finally upon us. Anuradha walked up to me.

'Hey, I'll leave now as well,' she said. 'Can you hand over my payment?'

I stared at her in silence.

Just then, someone walked up to me.

'Mini Shukla?' she said. 'Your boss is here.'

'Huh?' I said, trying to wrap my head around this idea. 'Who? Shipra?'

'No,' said the girl. 'See? He's with Vaishali.'

I turned around to see Vaishali walking towards us with Avinash. I didn't know how to react to this.

'Hello sir,' I croaked as they approached us. Avinash did not answer. He was looking at Anuradha.

'Avinash,' said Vaishali. 'I trust you have met our beautiful cover girl, Anuradha?'

Avinash appeared almost human as he took Anuradha's hand.

'I haven't had the pleasure,' he said, and hogwash to the tune of 'who ever loved that loved not at first sight' burnt bright in his eyes. He looked at Anuradha. He looked some more, and as it turned out, he was nowhere near done looking. Anuradha looked a little bemused at first at this unabashed gawping, but she was a seasoned celebrity, possibly used to having people stare.

'You can put that tongue back in your mouth,' she said with a laugh. Avinash blushed like a schoolboy with his first crush. He was still holding Anuradha's hand, which she removed politely after a minute of having it crushed in his paw. Vaishali and I exchanged looks.

'You are much prettier than you look in pictures,' he said. In Avinash's world, this was as close as one could get to an ode to beauty.

Vaishali coughed loudly at this point. Avinash turned to look at her.

'Yes, Vaishali?' he said, clearly not pleased at having to stop his looking.

'We need to discuss the advertising,' she said.

'Later!' he waved her away like a pesky mosquito.

'Oh alright,' said Vaishali and walked off in a huff. Now there were three.

'Let me take you out to dinner,' said Avinash. Anuradha stared at him. I stared at both, albeit from a distance.

'I'm sorry? What makes you think I would be interested?' she asked.

'Err, I'm looking for a new brand ambassador for our brand

Angel. I'd like to explain it to you,' said the quick thinker amongst us.

Anuradha thought for a moment and then shrugged.

'Alright,' she said. 'We can talk about it. Just a minute though. Mini, can I have my cheque before I leave?'

Avinash noticed me for the first time.

'What about this cheque, huh?' he barked at me.

'She needs to give me my cheque,' Anuradha explained.

Well, this was it. My prayers had been answered. Just when my career was about to be mud, the most unlikely person had come to my aid. I just needed to play this carefully.

'That's alright, Anuradha,' I said politely. 'Don't worry about the cheque. Sir will take care of it. Anyway, he is the final signing authority and not a penny moves out of JRE without his permission. Go on ahead with your, uh, meeting and he will settle your dues.'

Anuradha widened her eyes.

'Really? So you really are a big shot, eh?' she said playfully, but now taking him a little more seriously.

Avinash looked at me. I looked back innocently.

'He is the CEO,' I said, enunciating each letter carefully. Anuradha whistled appreciatively.

'Yes, yes,' he mumbled. 'Whatever it is, I will clear it. Let's just leave now.'

Anuradha left with Avinash after a quick air-kiss in my direction.

I was ecstatic at having wriggled out of a corner that Lardie had painted me into. I jumped up in the air and clicked my heels. Never again would I diss love at first sight. There was something to be said about malfunctioning hearts.

'Glad the shoot made you this happy,' said Rohan, emerging from the shadows, his bag full of cameras hanging on his shoulder.

'Ah but you flatter yourself,' I said. 'This is only a celebration of my powers to manipulate situations to my advantage.'

'Really?' he said doubtfully. 'Somehow you strike me as just the opposite, always unprepared, with absolutely no idea of the ball that you will play next.'

'Well thank you,' I said crossly. 'You were such a grump through the shoot and now you insult me.'

'Come, let me feed you,' he said with a laugh. 'To make up for trying to give my best to your critical cover shoot. You can insult me back.'

I considered this. Food over self-respect. It was an easy choice,

'Biryani,' I said, as we walked out of the studio.

# twelve

The day after the shoot, it could be said without an overstatement of facts that the Shukla girl reported to work a cheerful woman. It was a decidedly refreshing change from feeling like a wet dog all the time. I said a cheery hello to Mumu and quickly proceeded to my desk before she could remind me of her decision to catch Prakash red-handed.

Lardie was stuffed into her chair as usual, probably had been there since dawn. Feeling braver than usual, I walked up to her.

'Hi there. Care for some coffee and croissant with your beloved junior?' I said with an all-encompassing smile.

She looked up from her computer.

'Are you feeling alright?' she growled in my direction.

'Well, no need to be so sharp really,' I said cheerfully. 'I am just trying to be friendly.'

In response she muttered words how a girl with her upbringing had no business knowing and I had none understanding.

'I actually thought I would just let you know that the shoot was yesterday,' I said, unable to just leave well enough alone. 'It went off very well, you will be pleased to know.'

Lardie scowled at me.

'It's not over yet, my pet, let Anuradha turn up here demanding her dough and we will watch you meet your, eh, timely end,' said Lardie.

I responded with manic, booming laughter.

'Anuradha's payment is being looked after by the CEO,' I said gleefully. 'I'll let you know once the cheque is in the mail, which should be, let's see, right about now.'

With this I walked back to my desk. The phone rang as soon as I reached.

'Have you started preparing?' screeched Tanya.

Huh? I quickly racked my brains for what I was supposed to prepare for.

'The dance, the dance, the dance,' she shouted. 'Have you forgotten all about it, you dimwit?'

'No, of course not,' I laughed nervously. 'I was just very busy with the shoot, you know.'

'Well, the shoot is over and done with, is it not?' she demanded. 'You should be focusing on important things now. How'd the shoot go anyway?'

'Oh Tan,' I began, puffing up like a toad about to make a call to the ladies. 'It was brilliant. There were parrots…'

'Anyway,' she cut me off rudely, 'who are you bringing with you to the *sangeet*? You need a partner.'

So much for sensitive friends. I adopted a hurt tone.

'Well, I don't really have anyone in particular,' I said. 'Who would want to dance with me anyway?'

'Hmm, let me think about that,' she said, sounding very

stressed. 'Anyway, I have to go now. This stuff on my face is almost dry.'

I gulped.

'You are not really wearing a face mask sitting there at your desk, are you?' I asked.

'Of course not, silly! What sort of a crazed woman would wear a face mask at office?' she said. I heaved a sigh of relief.

'It's only bleach,' she continued and hung up.

Well, this dance routine was going to be a painful process. I tried to think of suitable men who could accompany me to the sangeet. After my bitter experience with Varun, I would have liked to go with a man I could trust. It was a pity Prithvi was the bridegroom. He would have been perfect. In my desperation, I scratched the underside of the bottom of the barrel now. Subbu! No, he would get drunk on the cocktails and start complimenting Tanya. Passions could run high at weddings and Prithvi was eminently capable of making Subbu forever keep his peace. Juggu! No, he liked to spend his spare time downing some *tharra* and listening to Bhojpuri songs. Gah! I had no man! No man! I was a man-less woman.

The phone rang.

'Hello?' I said morosely.

'You might as well sing a requiem,' said Rohan Vaidya.

'I am morose,' I announced.

'I figured. Listen, I was just looking at the photographs, and even though I do say it myself, they look great,' he said.

'Really? That's wonderful, Rohan,' I said, no longer

morose. 'Send them across right away, won't you? I can't wait to see them.'

'Yes, I'm sending a copy to *Azura* as well. You guys can coordinate about which picture will finally go on the cover,' he explained.

'Yeah baby! I mean, I will do so at the earliest, thanks,' I said.

He laughed.

'You sound upbeat this morning,' he said. 'I wish I had carefree youth on my side.'

I hastened to correct him.

'My life is not carefree, Rohan,' I said sadly. 'The shoot proceeding as per plan is the first positive thing to happen in a long time. And now I face the wrath of my best friend for not being able to perform at her wedding *sangeet*.'

'What's the issue?' he asked.

'Well, other than the fact that I look like a monkey reaching out for distant fruit when I am on the dance floor, I am also man-less. No partner,' I sighed.

'What are you saying? A drop-dead beauty like you should be able to find hundreds of suitors,' he mocked me.

'Mr Vaidya, I'm considered fairly attractive I will have you know,' I bristled. 'I just can't seem to find a date when I need one most, that's all. Also, smart alec comments at a moment like this are not appreciated too much.'

'I could go with you,' he said unexpectedly. 'If I am not too old for you, that is.'

I thought about this for a second. I had never gone out with a man who was more than five years my senior. And

Rohan? He was ancient, over the hills really.

'I am thirty-six, Mini,' he said, as if reading my mind. 'I hope that doesn't make me uncool or whatever the term you youngsters are using for "is like my parents".'

I laughed. For someone that old, he was still pretty sharp.

'Yeah okay,' I said, relieved at solving the problem. 'I hope you're not too embarrassed by Bollywood songs.'

'What are you saying? I thrive on them. You should see my Mithun steps,' he said.

'Sheesh, you really are getting on,' I said with a laugh and promised to call him to fix the time for our dance practice. This was really nice of him, I thought after I had hung up. Of course one could not go through life on the mercy of strangers and pity dates, but this was an exception.

I decided to stay out of Tanya's hair for the next few days while she sorted out the final details of the ceremony, only speaking when spoken to and being uncharacteristically pliable. I even found the time to practise some steps to 'Say na, say na, how you said it to me' at home. Urvashi encouraged me by walking into the room when I was rehearsing the supremely difficult 'dhol bajda' step and collapsing into giggles that lasted for a full twenty minutes. Menaka gave me a minor coronary by informing me that she had clean forgotten to give my blouse material to the tailor as requested by me six weeks ago and the fabric, contrary to my expectations, was not being cut and tailored to fit me but actually lying in her cupboard. After battling palpitations I managed to speak to a tailor at the JRE factory who promised to get his cousin, also a tailor, to do a rush job for me. All in all, it was turning out to be a great pre-wedding time, full of emergencies and disasters that we would laugh about a few years later but right now could only be termed overwhelming in every sense of the word.

My parents arrived a day before Tanya's *sangeet*. They both found me thin and lacking in health. When I informed them that I had actually gained three pounds gorging on office junk at all hours of the day and night, they tut-tutted and dismissed my claims. That evening I had the conversation I'd been expecting all along with my mother.

'So, Tanya's wedding is also taking place,' she said, putting down a cup of tea on my table.

'Only if all goes well,' I said, ironing the dress that I would be wearing the next day. 'Remember to hold your silence, Ma.'

'Heh heh,' she said. 'That Tanya is lucky. Prithvi is a very good boy. Both your Papa and I have always liked him. No vices, very respectable.'

I thought about the story that was currently doing the rounds about Prithvi's bachelor party. This story involved the bridegroom having a dozen shots of tequila off a bartender's navel — a bartender who was a hairy male. In Prithvi's defence, he claimed that he was stoned out of his mind and had no idea what he was doing.

No vices, indeed.

'Yes Ma,' I said. 'He is a very good boy.'

'You should also now find a good boy, beta,' Mom came to the point, 'and settle down.'

'Sure, Ma,' I said. 'I am on it.'

'No jokes, Mini,' said my mother sternly. 'You should be serious about these things. Trishna Aunty was saying that registering on wedding websites is very easy these days, no more newspaper matrimonial *jhamela*. I think that's very good. What do you think?'

'Ma! Trishna Aunty's darling daughter found someone in medical school and got married to him. What would she know about wedding sites?'

My mother sighed.

'Yes, medical school is very good. People find their life partners there all the time,' she declared sadly.

'Yeah,' I said sitting down next to her, 'and in their free time, they also learn a little medicine.' I put my head on my mother's lap.

'I've been having a very tough time at work, mother,' I said. 'Will you and Papa be terribly disappointed if I get fired?'

'*Hai*! Who will fire you? Their company will shut down if they fire you,' she said bravely. I listened to her take off on my employers and felt comforted by it.

'And even if you do get fired,' she continued, 'you can always come back home and we can use that time to register on some wedding websites. Trishna Aunty was saying everyone in America uses janamjanamkesaathi.com and that it is just wonderful.'

I groaned. It was apparent that getting fired was a bad idea for reasons less obvious to the naked eye. The other half of the parent-duo came into the room, looking well-fed and happy. He had just polished off the remnants of the fine meal that he had prepared for me.

'Mini, you should get a cook,' he said, 'someone to make you regular meals.'

'Or I could keep you here,' I said contemplatively.

'I am not retired yet,' he grumbled, 'and your mother won't let me consider chucking the job.'

'She needs a husband,' Mom interrupted.

'Only if he can cook,' said my father and took off his apron.

I went off to sleep tired. The weekend came too early for my comfort. The morning was full of confusion. Dad misplaced my mother's suitcase and spent the better part of an hour looking for it. Finally they were dressed and ready to leave. After packing off the parents to the venue in a taxi, I went to the parlour where Tanya was getting ready for her *sangeet*. She looked resplendent in a beautiful red salwar-kameez. Who could say what a monster hid beneath those beautiful clothes?

'I want six flowers on each side of my hair parting,' she snapped at the make-up professional.

'I will be so happy when you are finally married,' I said fervently, meaning every word I said.

She looked at me suspiciously and dialled someone's number on her mobile phone.

'Mumu! Where are you? I need those hairclips now! Yeah, get here as fast as you can,' she disconnected with the flair of a tyrant and turned to me to speak.

'So I have asked Varun to turn up for the *sangeet* to be your partner. I thought it would be a good way to make up for the incident with the pomegranate juice.'

I gawped at her in silence. Then I opened my mouth a couple of times to say something but no words could possibly express my incredulity.

'Gah,' I finally managed.

'You're welcome,' said Tanya with a toss of her pretty but oh-so-wicked head. 'I am looking great, I am looking hot, whoever thinks otherwise can go rot.'

I dreaded asking what she was doing but she caught my look.

'My bridal reaffirmation,' she explained, and pouted for her third coat of lipstick.

'That's okay,' I wailed, 'but what about Varun? What about me? I don't want to have anything to do with him.'

'Don't stress me out,' she snapped and then tried a simpering smile in the mirror. The make-up artist rolled her eyes.

'I am the one under stress here,' I grumbled. 'I wish you'd checked with me once, Tanya.'

'Checked for what? You didn't have a date, Varun is the only guy I could think of who would be willing to go out with you. Also, I must start my married life with a clean slate. Wipe out all my sins, you know? Check my third upper eyelash, will you?' she said and turned to the immensely patient make-up lady.

'That's the thing, Tanya. I *do* have a date. I called Rohan Vaidya and he is coming and I don't know what I will tell him and I don't know what I will tell Varun and it's all going to be so weird,' I paused for a breath, feeling miserable.

'You have a date? Why didn't you say so? And isn't Rohan

Vaidya a golden oldie?' she asked in an exasperated voice. I bristled at this.

'He is old but not bad at all. And what was I supposed to do. You had a gun to my head about this *sangeet*,' I cried. 'I just agreed to go with the first person who would have me.'

'Yeah, maybe,' she said uncertainly. 'So what should I do now? Should I call Varun and ask him not to come? What should I do? Maybe I should call and apologise to Varun.' The make-up artist touched her on the shoulder lightly at this point to communicate that she was done. 'AM I READY? REALLY READY? READY TO LEAVE?' The make-up artist nodded, looking relieved that this indeed was the case.

'Nothing,' I said, also getting up. 'I'll handle it. I don't want you to get into any mess today, do you hear? Just focus on getting married before Prithvi sees the light of day. It's your *sangeet*, just go and do what brides do, be temperamental and expect the world to bow to your whims.'

'Alright, yes, I must control my control-freakishness,' she demurred and we made our way out to the car that was waiting to ferry us to the venue of the *sangeet*. The venue looked beautiful. I noticed that there was plenty of absolutely delicious and exotic-looking foods doing the rounds and there were flowers floating about in carved silver urlis. I met Tanya's parents, who lived abroad, and had come to Mumbai only a few days back before the wedding — as instructed by Tanya. They told me they were stunned at how she had everything under control. I merely smiled and nodded.

Tanya was deposited at the small stage where the *dholak-waali* and the professional folk-singers and *mehendi-waali* sat. She blossomed under all their attention. I decided to get something to drink and went off to the stall giving out gorgeously decorated mocktails.

'It's surprising how we always meet at the water cooler, eh?' said Varun from behind me. I stifled an oath and turned around. He was wearing a sherwani and looked absolutely edible.

'Heh heh, yeah,' I said and took a sip of the pineapple drink to steady myself before I could tell him about my prior engagement with Rohan, and immediately wished that it contained something significantly stronger.

'You look like you could do with some Dutch courage,' he said, moving closer. I hastily edged away.

'Oh, there's Mini,' I heard my mother say as she caught sight of me. Tanya's mother was with her, clutching the excel sheet that Tanya had handed to her to refer to for the schedule of the evening.

'*Beta*, come, you need to start the performance section as Tanya has termed it,' she said, and then saw who was with me. Curiosity wiped out the last vestige of urgency that she had come to me with.

'I don't think I recognise him,' she told me, nodding fervently at him.

'Mom, you cannot recognise him because you have never met him,' I said, exasperated. 'Varun works with Tanya and me.' Mom smiled broadly at Varun, taking in his expensive clothes and good looks.

'Very nice, *beta*. Come, come, have some drinks,' Tanya's mother assessed my mother's approval of the lad and hastened to help. Varun dimpled at both of them. I groaned inwardly and then caught sight of my father absentmindedly nodding at something that Tanya's father was telling him. I left Varun with the ladies and walked up to him.

'Papa,' I hissed, 'get Mom away from that boy. I want to have nothing to do with him.'

'Huh? Which boy?' said Papa, looking befuddled before his eyes settled on Varun. 'Ah, yes, there's a boy with your mother.' He walked up to them.

There was a tap on my shoulder.

'Hi there,' said Rohan. 'Sorry I'm a little late.'

'Gah,' I said, startled. 'No, that's okay.' I saw that Tanya's mother and my parents had started walking towards me with Varun in tow.

'Arrey, it's okay, sweetheart,' said my father. 'This is only Varun, the boy who is going to perform in the dance with you. Mom says you invited him.'

Rohan's face rapidly lost colour, like a vegetable dye kurta washed in strong detergent.

'Uh, I guess I'll take your leave then,' he said and started to walk away. This was all wrong.

'No, Rohan, wait,' I said but my mother pulled me back.

'Mini, Varun is a designer in your company,' she informed me.

'I work with him, Ma, I know,' I said and ran after Rohan. He was wearing a kurta-pyjama, attire decidedly different from what I was accustomed to seeing him in.

'Ugh, stop stomping off,' I told him when I caught up with him, breathless. 'No need for this drama. I can explain.'

He smiled. 'There's nothing to explain,' he said. 'I know

how these things work. You found someone who was better suited for your purpose and you forgot to tell me, that's all.'

'Stop making me sound like Matahari,' I told him. 'Tanya called Varun because she thought I wouldn't be able to wrangle a date.'

He suddenly grinned. 'Oh well, in that case, this is decision time for you, my friend,' he said. A small girl came up to me.

'Tanya didi has told me to tell you that you better make up your mind and get your ass up on the stage at once or you are dead meat,' she said and ran off.

'Damn!' I said eloquently and left Rohan to walk up to where Varun was standing, patiently waiting for me to return.

'Hey Varun,' I said as casually as I could manage. 'The thing is, why don't you just hang about or something? I already asked Rohan to dance with me at this *sangeet* before Tanya spoke to you. We've even practised together. You're not missing out on much anyway. I'm a terrible dancer.'

The change on Varun's face was almost comical. He looked positively destroyed. He pursed his lips and looked away in the distance for a full minute, possibly trying to not lose his temper. Then apparently a little more in control of his emotions, he turned back and asked, 'Why?'

'Why what?' I sought an elaboration.

'Why are you doing this to me?' he asked.

'I am not doing anything to you, man,' I said, watching out for Tanya who might be walking up to me any moment with a cat o' nine tails in her hand.

'You led me on,' he accused me.

'I most certainly did not,' I said, furious, my focus completely on him now.

'You appeared so concerned when I got drunk on the juice,' he said.

'That was because Tanya had spiked it, you moron!' I shouted before I could control myself.

His face whitened.

'You're lying!' he said. 'Why would Tanya call me here if she did not like me? Why would she spike my juice?

'I am not lying.' Now I really was on a spree, having thrown all discretion to the winds. 'She wanted to punish you for your hidden girlfriend. Oh yes, Mr Casanova, we know all about her. That's why Mumu and Prithvi followed you. They. Saw. You. Kissing. So now why don't you tell me who the liar is?'

'My god,' Varun was speechless for a second. 'She was the one who spiked my juice! I will have her fired!'

Belatedly I realised that I had said too much.

'Go back to your girlfriend, Varun,' I said quietly. 'And if you need variety, approach your good friend Shipra.'

Varun was clearly flabbergasted. He looked at me again, shook his head and walked off. Then he turned around.

'It's not my fault,' he said. 'You've got it all wrong. I am not the one treating anyone like shit.'

I shrugged. He walked out.

'Everything alright?' asked Rohan when I walked back to him. 'That was quite a scene you had there with the good-looking gentleman.'

'Let's go and get this done,' I said and led the way to the dance floor. Much applause greeted us from all quarters as we shimmied to the songs selected by Tanya. Rohan was no better than me as far as dancing skills were concerned, but together we provided the cheering crowds with plenty of entertainment.

'That was brilliant,' said Tanya when we got off the dance floor. 'Thanks for doing this for me, Mini! You were fantastic!'

I looked at her and felt guilt overcome me. For her wedding gift, I was getting her fired.

# thirteen

Tanya's wedding, held only a day after the *sangeet*, sped by in a blur of silk clothes I was not accustomed to, heavy jewellery that made my neck cramp, and consequent compliments that I was most certainly not used to. The other thing that I was not familiar with was the heavy shroud of guilt that covered me at all times. Tanya had no idea that Varun knew all about her brilliant plot of adding a little more than just love and good wishes to his juice. In my typical discreet fashion I had decided to keep certain facts to myself till after the wedding and honeymoon. It would give me ample time to come up with a plan to handle the consequences of my little outburst at the *sangeet*.

The wedding day passed without incident, not counting the tantrum that Tanya threw first thing in the morning because the tea served to her was not just right. When it was time to exchange garlands, Prithvi teasingly refused to bow down enough for her to reach him. She promptly stomped him on his foot, causing to bend down in a hurry. The *pheras* were done and the bride and groom sat down to have dinner as wedded partners. I gave them company.

'I can have real food again,' said Tanya as she dug into a gulab-jamun. 'No more diets. I was a slim bride and I have the pictures to prove it. Now, pass me the pastries.'

'At least wait till the honeymoon is over, Tan. At this rate you will not even fit into all the expensive lingerie that you have bought for the trip,' I said as I saw her pile chocolate meringues on her plate. Prithvi coughed next to me and shook his head slightly. Apparently the honeymoon was a taboo topic. Tanya caught him gesturing to me.

'What are you shaking your head at her for?' she demanded. 'She should know the first act of foolishness and insensitivity you've committed as my legally wedded husband.'

'Well, I'm willing to put my neck on the line as long as you're willing to support me,' Pri retorted with a grin and turned to me.

'We can't leave on our honeymoon immediately,' he explained. 'There is this really critical project that has come up at work and I need to be here to man it. The office was very apologetic but if I am to get that promotion, I can't go on leave now. In her usual understanding fashion, Tanya here thinks it's an unforgivable tear in the fabric of our marital bliss, brought about solely in order to cause her immeasurable grief and untold pain.'

'Of course I do. Now I will have to reschedule my leave, not that I am doing any work anyway,' Tanya began to argue. Their voices faded out as the bells of my own misfortune started to peal loudly in my ears.

Tanya was not leaving immediately. That meant that she would turn up at work … when? Next week?

'So when do you come back to work, Tan?' I asked as casually as I could.

'Tomorrow,' she said causing me to pale underneath the thick layer of make-up that I was wearing in order to look pretty.

'Heh heh, surely not?' I fumbled.

She looked at me coldly. 'I am. There's no point taking leave when all I will do is stay at home and wait for His Crappiness to arrive from work,' she said in a remarkable display of bridal coyness and romantic love.

'Yes, yes, of course,' I hastily smoothed her ruffled feathers.

'Though what I will do there now that the wedding's done is anyone's guess,' she continued to grumble as she dug into some more cake. After the bride had had her fill of carbohydrates, the party was declared over. Tanya and Prithvi retired to the hotel room presumably to consummate their marriage though they looked like they needed sleep more than sex. In the mentioned room they must have found evidence of their friends' sophisticated and classy sense of humour in the form of condoms filled with water.

I landed at the office the next day a shadow of my former ebullient self. It could even be said that I was not bringing sunshine wherever I went. In the circles lining my otherwise shiny eyes, there was definite evidence of a night spent tossing. Also turning.

Lardie was sitting at her desk with Varun perched at the edge of the table when I walked in. Both of them had evidently been discussing the events that featured me in the starring role because they shut up and started looking in different directions as soon as they caught sight of me.

I tried to ignore them and sat down at my desk. Maybe if I focused on the problem with a clear mind, a solution would emerge. I had some time before things started to heat up. I started my computer and logged in to check for new mails. The phone rang.

'Bat's calling you,' said Mumu. One could describe her voice as hollow and one would be considered accurate. 'There's going to be trouble.'

'Already? I haven't even had time to stretch the old noggin for some brilliance,' I said in a quivering voice. Mumu laughed, still sticking with hollowness and hung up.

I got up to go for my funeral. Varun was no longer sitting at Lardie's desk, I noticed. Mumu waved me inside Bat's office. I knocked and walked in. Bat was sitting at his desk, signing some papers that Prakash was holding out for him. Varun sat in one of the couches.

Nobody said anything. There was another knock and Tanya walked in. She looked remarkably sleepy. She looked at me and raised a questioning eyebrow. I didn't say anything. Varun looked away steadfastly. Bloody tattle-tale, I thought darkly to myself. Finally, Bat walked over to the sitting area. Prakash lurked in the background.

'So, what the hell has been going on here?' Bat started in his usual polished fashion.

Tanya and I kept quiet. Varun took a deep breath and started to speak.

'I am in evidence of the fact that certain members of

this organisation have been partly or totally responsible for causing a state of inebriation in certain other members of the same organisation, thereby causing disruption during the deliverance of the latter's duties,' he said. Bat stared at him. We all stared at him.

'Did a lawyer bite you in the morning?' Bat barked at Varun who crumpled in his seat.

'I think what he means is that Tanya spiked his drink,' said Prakash, a smirk on his face. Tanya gasped. I stared at the carpet.

'Wha…' said Tanya and then proceeded into a 'Howwwww' before petering out into a 'Buttttttttt'. I wanted to reach out and hold her hand but decided that I was better off continuing to memorise the pattern on the carpet.

'Yes, sir. That is what I wanted to say,' said Varun, relieved that Prakash had taken on the onus of divulging the details.

'How do you know?' demanded Bat of Varun.

'She told me!' said Varun and pointed a finger at me to avoid any confusion.

Tanya gaped at me, her mouth slightly open. Prakash smirked some more. Bat turned to me.

'You! Did you?' Bat turned on me. I contemplated outright denial as a means of escape and then ruefully rejected it as unfeasible. I nodded miserably.

'What the hell,' erupted Tanya, forgetting that she was in the presence of the bat creature that would decide her immediate to medium-term future and that swearing in his face was perhaps not the best way to corporate glory. Specially since he had clearly clean forgotten that she worked in the company.

'You told him?' she turned on me. I nodded again without looking up.

'Hmph,' said Tanya in my direction and puffed up her cheeks, a sure sign that she was very, very upset.

'So let me get this straight before you waste any more of my time on this HR shit … where is that asinine John Peters anyway?' Bat looked at Prakash.

'He's no more in our employment, sir,' reminded Prakash.

'Ah yes, that's always a good idea, firing asses like him.' Bat looked pleased with himself and then remembered that that as a consequence he was expected to sort out the mess that was currently sitting in his office.

'Why did you spike this moron's juice?' he asked of Tanya, nodding in Varun's direction.

'He totally deserved it, Mr A,' said Tanya. 'He is a cheat and a cad.'

'I'm not!' screamed Varun. 'It's not my fault! I can explain. My girlfriend…'

'Shut up,' said the Bat calmly. 'I have no time for all this personal crap.'

He turned to Tanya.

'You brought alcohol into the office and then used it to get him into some serious trouble. You are fired. Get out,' he said, causing Tanya to fall back into the chair, and then he turned to Varun.

'Last warning. No messing around with office chicks. Next time it's your bottom and my boot,' he said and then turned to me.

'What are you doing here?' he asked me, looking thoroughly puzzled.

'I … uh … nothing. I thought I would be needed,' I said, and then decided to add a few words, 'I'm sorry about what happened. It was probably my fault.'

'Well then, if you are feeling guilty enough, feel free to submit your resignation. Now, out everyone,' he said. Dismissed, we all trooped out, a collection of long faces and hang-dog expressions.

'Tan! Listen to me, it just slipped out at your *sangeet*,' I tried to explain as I followed Tanya to the basement. 'That bloody Varun wouldn't take no for an answer and I didn't want to cause a scene at your *sangeet*. You're very scary when you're upset.'

'Yeah, yeah, I'm listening,' she said absently as she called someone on the phone. I listened in to her side of the conversation.

'Hello Pri,' she said. 'I got fired!'

'Yeah, it sucks.'

'Hmm, mmm, well, they figured that it was I who got Varun drunk. Your beloved Mini lost her famous temper and told him at the *sangeet*.'

'Oh yes, I plan to kill her.'

'No, I don't regret it at all. In fact, I'd do it again in a second!'

'I guess so. Well, I thought I would let you know. You might need to support an unemployed wife for a while. Also, I might end up being unfaithful to you, what with so much free time on my hands.'

'Yes, we can talk about it in the evening. Bye for now.'

She sat down heavily in her chair and looked at me with Labrador eyes.

'I lost my job on the first day of my married life. This is a bad turn of events,' she said.

I nodded. 'Yeah,' I said. 'But look at it this way, you don't have to hand over anything to anyone.'

'Well, aren't you the supportive one today?' she said and started to take out some folders and files from her shelf.

'I'm really sorry, I am,' I said. 'And I will help you look for a new job with everything I have got.'

'Yes, I know,' she said and took out some visiting cards. 'Fat lot of good that will be, with Asha Lata not even taking calls these days.'

'Let's update your résumé tonight,' I said with an admirable touch of proactiveness.

'No need to update anything. All I have done in months and months is wedding planning,' she said. 'Look at all this stuff,' she pointed at the mess surrounding her. '*Mehendi-waali* database, flower arrangement ideas, shamiana designs, caterers — every single major supplier in this city catalogued and rated by yours truly.'

'I guess this is what it takes to have the kind of perfect wedding that you did,' I said. 'I'm going to outsource my own wedding, unlikely as that event is, to you.'

'It's odd that you should say that,' she said as she looked for a box to dump her belongings into. 'Three other women said the same thing to me at the wedding. I don't know what about this scares girls so much. I loved doing it. I could do it for the rest of my life. It's a pity everyone gets just one wedding on an average. Maybe Pri will divorce and remarry me.'

We both looked at each other in silence. I would have liked to report here that the epiphany was marked by the sun bursting through grey clouds and harps playing in the heavens above but it was not.

In reality, I told her, 'You should be a professional wedding planner.'

She looked a little stricken, not at all like a person whose dream job had just been delivered at her doorstep.

'You will be a great planner,' I said. 'All that bullying of suppliers, the incessant chase for the perfect outfits, the obsession with details...'

'You're right,' she said, warming to the idea. 'Maybe I'll make a few phone calls tonight to the people who had expressed interest in my ... uh ... skills.'

'You will be awesome. I know it. In fact I wish I could give you my business immediately to start you off, but what with the complete lack of any eligible men in my life...' I expressed my unequivocal support.

'Well, now that you mention it, your dancing king was not half bad. In fact, one could go as far as to say that together you constituted one whole pair of feet,' she said with a grin.

'Huh? Rohan? What nonsense! He's so elderly,' I said with a laugh that dismissed any notions that Tanya may have had about any romantic linkages existing between the good photographer and me.

'Um mm,' she said and let it go. I helped her pack her

solitary plant that had miraculously survived its period in the basement.

'I better go now,' I said. 'Lardie must have collected heaps of garbage for me to sort through.'

'She must be delighted that Varun and you had a falling out,' said Tanya as I edged out of her cubicle.

'There was no falling in to begin with,' I said. 'I hope that he flits endlessly between the mysterious girlfriend and Lardie, causing the latter inordinate amounts of heartache. Also heartburn.' With a final grimace I walked out.

What a terrible day this was turning out to be, I thought to myself as I sat in my chair and started to go through the meaningless trash-cleaning Lardie had lined up for me. The wedding was over. Tanya had been fired. There would be no one sitting under shamianas and no one calling all shapes and sizes of wedding suppliers over. This was tragic and it was entirely my fault. The only consolation seemed to be that Tanya would finally be out of the job that had rendered her so jobless that she was able to find a new vocation for herself.

And at least the shoot was over, I thought to myself. I had carefully selected the picture from the several contained in the CD that Rohan had sent over. It showed Anuradha holding a parrot in one hand, the bird fluttering its wings merrily while she smiled beatifically at the reader. The Angel clothes looked great and the brand's logo was visible at her shoulder where everyone could see it and remember to buy the gorgeous, yet affordable garments. I had even assessed whether the inspiration from Bollywood was evident and had decided that it was. I had confirmed with Zoya that Anuradha had spoken about her love and admiration for the brand in the interview, and while she had admitted to me that the shoot was the first time that she had ever even seen Angel clothes, she sounded quite convincing, said Zoya.

Yes, it was a good picture. I hoped it would look good on the cover.

# fourteen

The next two weeks were largely uneventful, and for this, the *ghar ka chiraag* of the Shukla *khandaan* was mighty grateful. Varun and Lardie started spending more and more time together, and I thanked my stars. Lardie was clearly in the throes of love and took to wearing fuchsia pink dresses to office. She often forgot to give me work and it was clear that I stood to benefit from the first blush of her romance with the cad. I was quite certain that Varun had not told her about the lady he was officially betrothed to, but with the aid of hindsight acquired after getting my best friend fired, I knew that flying below the radar was the best strategy.

While I still suffered from the occasional pang of guilt when it came to the aforementioned best friend, she seemed to have taken to the wedding planning business like a baboon to a banana. The first wedding project was in place and Tanya had already started using the advance to print visiting cards, which depicted her sitting under a shamiana. She thought they were cute. Prithvi and I battled nausea but did not offer comment.

Urvashi took to getting home an unsavoury character that

sported long hair, cheap roadside earrings in both ears and loud, tight t-shirts on his person, and after I found myself walking in nearly every evening to a house that smelt of grass that was not green anymore, I started seriously contemplating finding myself new flatmates, if not a new flat. Having potheads as potential rent-free housemates was where I drew the line.

In some parts of the country, winter set in. Mumbai, never having cared for this earth getting farther from the sun and cooling down business, continued to be hot and occasionally hotter. The festival season was right around the corner. People were falling out of the malls and shops. It was a busy time for business.

It was at around this time that the November edition of *Azura* hit the stands.

It started innocently enough, as such things often do.

I was in a taxi that was taking me to work when I saw a magazine vendor approach the car.

I shooed him away before I heard him advertising his wares.

'Latesht Azoora, maydum,' he informed me. *'Yeh dekhiye.'*

I took a look and gasped. Sure enough, there was Anuradha and the parrot, gracing the cover of the glossy. I hastily took out a hundred-rupee note and, thrusting it into the startled vendor's hands, snatched the magazine that would determine the course of my career.

Anuradha was smiling. The clothes looked gorgeous. The parrot looked as happy as a parrot posing for a fashion picture could look. 'Anuradha Menon — the star of the modelling world talks about life, love and lust,' screamed the headline.

And yet...

...there was something wrong.

It took me a moment to realise what was amiss in the picture and then I briefly contemplated asking the cabbie to take me to the emergency ward of the nearest hospital, so certain was I of the coronary arrest that was currently somewhere in the region of my palpitating heart.

The Angel logo on the shoulder of Anuradha's top had been covered by text. Where there should have been a smiling angel with a halo around its blonde curls, there was now large red letters suggesting '10 ways to tell him you've moved on. With his best friend'.

'Gah,' I said.

'Gawph,' I elaborated.

'Garumph,' I finished.

I gulped loudly, took another look at the magazine, and then a few steadying, deep breaths. I turned to the page where Anuradha had been interviewed by the magazine. I quickly scanned through the words to reach the part where she had talked about Angel.

'...and I love Angle. The clothes are just gorgeous. They do amazing skirts and...'

*Angle?* As in the figure formed by two lines diverging from a common point? Not Angel, a benevolent celestial being that acts as an intermediary between heaven and earth, sharing his name with the brand that I served?

Oh my goodness. I quickly read the rest of the article and, sure enough, every single time there was an Angle staring me in the face.

This was bad.

Very, very bad.

Irrevocably bad.

What should I do now? What were my options? The Arabian Sea stretched nearby and drowning was supposedly quite painless. I quickly dismissed that option and forced myself to think of the positive side. I thought for five minutes and there was no positive to it at all. It was just tons and tons of negative stuff oozing all over my résumé.

No, wait.

Maybe I was too close to the entire project to be a good judge of the true magnitude of the problem. Maybe it was not such a huge issue after all. Maybe the others, specially Avinash, would not even notice that the logo was hidden and the brand name misspelt? Yes, maybe that would be the case. I was just overreacting. My heart stopped behaving like the Shatabdi Express trying to make up for lost time and settled into a normal lub-dub beat.

The phone rang. It was Rohan.

'Hi! I saw the magazine,' I said, forcing myself to sound cheerful.

'I'm so sorry, Mini,' he said in a morose tone.

'Nah, it's okay,' I said. 'I'm sure it happens all the time. It does, doesn't it?'

'Of course not!' he said. 'This is terrible. Your brand! The damage! This is insane! How could they do this? You should sue them!'

I gulped.

'Rohan, do you think my boss will be very upset?' I asked,

my nerves standing at end.

'Of course he will! I would be furious!' he then remembered that my relations with my boss were far from congenial. 'I mean, of course he will understand that none of this is your fault, Mini. Don't worry. Just thrash it out with him and decide on the best course of action.'

'Yes, I will but I need to go now,' I stuttered as the taxi pulled up in front of my office building. I arrived at my floor and saw a long-faced Mumu at her station. I looked down at her desk to find the magazine in her hands.

'Heh heh,' I said nervously. 'Nice cover, eh?'

Mumu looked up.

'He's asked you to come into his office as soon as you arrive,' she said in a dull voice. 'Things are going from bad to worse.'

'Uff, stop being such a harbinger of doom, Mumu,' I said as I edged away from the vicinity of Avinash's office as fast as I could. Before I was done edging away, though, Prakash emerged from the shadows that had hitherto concealed him.

'Ah, the star of the day has arrived!' he said in a jovial tone. 'Please do step inside. We have been waiting forever.' Since gulping seemed to be the activity of the day, I gulped again, this time very loudly.

'Ha ha, I will just go to my desk and see you in a minute,' I said, making a quick but strong decision to make a getaway to New Zealand as soon as I could steal a couple of moments to myself.

'That won't be convenient for Avinash, no,' said Prakash,

almost meditatively. 'Right this way, if you don't mind, and at once.'

I shot a despairing look at Mumu and she bade me farewell with misty eyes. I stepped inside Avinash's cabin.

He had the magazine open in front of him and was gazing adoringly at Anuradha. Prakash sidled up to him and informed him that he had company. Avinash looked up and found me cowering in a corner.

'Where is the logo?' he asked quietly. Prakash sidled out.

'Oh, logo, heh heh, looks like it's hiding right there, behind the words "10 ways". In fact, if you look really, really closely, perhaps a magnifying glass is in order, you will even spot the curls of the angel in our logo, heh heh,' I petered out.

'Curls? Do you think I am a loon? An insane piece of shit? A moron who is better off inside a padded cell?' he asked. I replied in the negative, sacrificing honesty for tact.

'Then how the hell do you think you can get away with showing a curl where I should have a big, bold logo? Where is my logo? My logo? Did I not pay money for the logo? Should I not be seeing the logo? Am I wrong in asking for the logo? Where is the bloody logo?' he bellowed. I told him that I would be unable to help him with the same, given that the logo was in fact not visible on the cover.

'What the hell are you getting a salary for when you can't even ensure a visible logo? And Angle? Angle? I will tell you what the angle to this story is — the angle is that a stupid piece of shit has disguised herself as the brand bloody manager,' he screamed, his cheeks turning a florid red and a pulse beating furiously in his temple. I took a deep breath for both of us and launched into an explanation.

'Look, I know it's a mistake. Let me just go and speak to the magazine. I am sure Vaishali will make it good,' I said. 'It's a great picture, you will agree. Just a couple of loose ends that I need to tie.'

'Shut up! Stop blabbering!' for a moment I thought he would hit me and started to edge away again. 'If I wanted to see Anuradha looking good in pictures, I would just look at them on my computer. Ahem, I mean, Anuradha will look good anywhere. Anyway, the point is that I paid good money to get this brand coverage and now something called an Angle has angled all the bloody attention and all I am left with is the bloody bills. All because you were a moron.' I continued to cower in my corner. This was not turning out to be the thrashing-out that Rohan had had in mind.

'Get out! Out!' he yelled. 'Out of my face, out of my office, out of my company! I should have never trusted you to accomplish a simple task such as this. Get out! Ooooout!'

'I am going, I am going,' I said hastily and started towards the door when it burst open and Tanya spilled in, breathless and panicked. She waved her arms about frantically.

'What the bloody...' said a startled Avinash.

'Mumu ... Prakash ...' gasped Tanya.

'What are you doing here?' I asked Tanya.

'Came to ... collect ... dues ... Mumu ... in danger ... let's go,' managed Tanya and ran back out of the same door. I looked at Avinash, uncertain about the next step.

'I guess we better see what she's huffing and puffing about,' said Avinash in a most leader-like fashion, and started to lead the way out as leaders are wont to do.

As soon as we got out of the cabin, we caught sight of Tanya's red dupatta turning a fast and furious corner.

'There she is,' I screamed and gave chase. 'I know that dupatta. It's mine. She borrowed it last month and never gave it back.'

'Shut up, shut up, shut up,' chanted Avinash as lugged his forty extra kilos and tried to keep up with Tanya. We were not too far behind her now.

She seemed to be running for the basement, I realised, as she took the staircase and started bounding down two steps at a time.

'Try to keep up,' she shouted up at me.

'I'm trying, I'm trying, can you tell me what the hell is going on?' I screamed down at her.

'My reputation is being flushed down the toilet,' commented Avinash as he nearly knocked down two boys from the kitchen as they climbed up the stairs bearing trays of steaming hot upma. My stomach growled.

'All this exercise on an empty stomach,' I yelled at Tanya. 'You better have a good reason, young lady.'

'Here we are!' she shouted back triumphantly as we reached the supplies closet.

'Now, everyone,' said Tanya, 'be prepared!' With these words, she kicked the door open. We all burst inside.

It took me a moment to adjust my eyes to the scene inside.

Prakash was lying stomach down on a table. Mumu was sitting on top of Prakash. Then I noticed that she had twisted one of his arms behind his back and, going by his periodic yowls, was currently causing him inordinate amount of pain.

'Leggo!' he screamed as he saw us enter.

'Thank god you're here,' Mumu said in relief.

'What is going on here? Mumtaaz? Prakash?' said a shocked Avinash. He walked up to the phone and dialled a number.

'Hello, Security? Come down to the basement at once. It is a code one. Code three. The code that means it's an emergency at any rate,' he said and turned to face the party.

'Let go of him,' he ordered Mumu. Mumu twisted Prakash's arm one final time and then let him go. He stood up slowly and rubbed his arm.

'What a monster,' he said and smoothed back his ruffled hair.

'He tried to get away so I sat on him and twisted his arm,' offered Mumu by way of an explanation.

'But why were you trying to hold him back?' asked Avinash, more bewildered by the moment. There was a knock at the door and a security guard came inside, looking very happy to be of some use other than making challans for clothes going out of the building. Avinash nodded at him to stay outside the door.

'He doesn't know,' whispered Mumu conspiratorially to me.

'Gah, *I* don't know either,' I said, completely exasperated.

'Don't believe them, sir,' pleaded Prakash, whose oil seemed to have washed away.

'I can decide once I know what she has to say,' said Avinash and turned to Mumu. 'I will throttle you if you don't tell us what's going on at once.'

'Well, the thing is this,' said Mumu, assuming her Poirot air at once, 'this man is an internet auction site addict.'

'Huh?' said Avinash and I in unison.

'What does that mean?' asked Avinash finally.

'It started off innocently enough,' explained Mumu patiently, 'with Prakash here registering on the website www.goinggoinggone.com. To start with, he bid for a carton of olive oil. To his delight, he won. The excitement started to seep into his system. He started getting used to the idea of winning. Soon, he was spending all his time bidding for things that he did not need. Just because he could.'

Prakash hung his head down further. It looked like Mumu was actually on the right track here.

'However, as happens with most addictions, money started dwindling. Prakash had bought CDs, a red bicycle, forty-two audio speakers of all shapes and sizes and a pet iguana that is being shipped to him as we speak,' continued Mumu. 'What he did not have was the money to support his addiction. He had no one who could lend him money without asking some uncomfortable questions. He was desperate. He needed to bid and win at all costs. He could not let this go for a simple reason like want of money! '

'So what did he do?' asked Avinash, interested in spite of himself.

'He did what most addicts in his situation end up doing,' said Mumu dramatically, 'he started stealing things.'

Here Mumu paused.

'Stealing? From where? His home?' I asked.

'He lives in paying guest digs and there's not much to grab there except faded curtains and ragged couches,' said Mumu.

'So where did he steal from? What did he do?' I asked.

'Well, the answer to Prakash's problem lay right next to him. He used the computer in this closet, a perfect hideaway where people hardly came, preferring to use the bigger supplies cabinet on the fourth floor of the building instead. In fact, Mini ended up coming this way and stumbling upon his little hideout only because Tanya sat in the basement as per, err, your orders, sir. Anyway, so this was the time that Prakash discovered the cupboard in the supplies closet, full of things, lovely, lovely things. Pens, paper from A1 to A6 with 2, 3, 4 and 5 thrown in for good measure, pencils, erasers, staplers ... and...'

'And?' Avinash and I asked in unison.

In response, Mumu walked over to one of the cupboards and flung open a cupboard.

'Used computers!' she declared with what could definitely be called a flourish. The cupboard had about twenty laptops stocked cheek by jowl in the cupboard. Some of them had post-its on them, stating the complaint that had rendered them useless. 'Does not follow QWERTY' — said one of them mysteriously.

'Huh?' responded Avinash, sharp as a button.

'As per the rules of the company, old and dysfunctional computers are replaced by new ones when the IT department deems fit, but they are sold off only once every year, at the end of the financial year,' said Mumu.

'Yes, I made that rule,' said Avinash.

'Resultantly, all the non-working laptops are stored here after they are declared unfit and here they wait for March when they can be sold off and see their new homes,' said Mumu.

Prakash tried to slink out of the room and Tanya deftly stood between him and the door. Defeated, he sat down in a chair.

'I think Prakash found out that used computers were kept in here quite by accident. But once he did, it was child's play for him to access the duplicate keys to this cupboard from the CEO's cabin. Then, within a matter of days, he took to auctioning off the laptops so he could have the money that he needed to buy useless junk. He started selling them off on the bidding site, one at a time. When the time for shipping came, he would leave his own laptop behind and smuggle one of the old machines out in his laptop bag. He has managed to rob the company of about five such laptops in the last few months,' ended Mumu.

Avinash shook his head in wonder and amazement.

'The things that go on in this office,' he said. 'How did you find all this out, Mumtaaz?'

Mumu smiled secretively.

'Nothing that a clever sleuth cannot uncover with the aid of a strategically placed video camera,' she declared.

'Did you really put a camera in here?' I asked.

'Well, I had to follow the money, right? I knew that the secret lay somewhere in this closet and so one night I slipped in and put in a little device,' she explained. 'It recorded Prakash coming in and taking out a computer from here. From there I just worked backwards.'

'But what tipped you off?' asked Avinash.

'Well, we knew that it must be related to what Prakash was doing on the computer when Mini walked into this closet — he was very startled and behaved guiltily and that would be the case only if he had been surfing a website that he shouldn't have. A quick word with the IT department helped me to find out his website history. All I can say is, when I saw a lot of goinggoinggone.com, I was quite surprised. I expected something quite different, if you know what I mean,' said Mumu and looked very pleased with herself.

I coughed discreetly. Mumu remembered where she was and blushed a deep shade of crimson.

'I was always on the lookout for any unusual behaviour from Prakash,' she continued. 'Soon I realised that sometimes he carried a laptop home even when his own was lying at his desk. An error to not hide it in the drawers, of course. The auction website, the laptop and the closet. I had these clues. He threatened Mini and Tanya, so it was also evident that what he was doing was criminal in nature and had to be concealed by him at all costs. With a little help from a wad of courier receipts from all over the world showing shipping of strange objects to him, I was able to put this jigsaw together.'

Avinash turned to Prakash.

'Prakash,' he said and seemed to be quite unable to say more.

'Prakash,' he repeated and was quite overcome with the effort.

'I will tender my resignation at once,' said the once oily Prakash in a mopey voice.

'That won't be necessary,' said Avinash. 'I am firing you. We will not report the matter to the police provided you seek rehab, if rehab for this sort of thing exists, that is.'

Poor Prakash. He did not say a word and kept looking at his shoes, a shadow of the man who had threatened us in the parking lot that day. I knew what he must be feeling, having been fired myself less than an hour back. There were now three ex-employees in the group, quite outnumbering the two who could roam the corridors without fear of being apprehended by the man in blue posted outside the door.

Avinash sighed loudly, doubtless feeling the burden of leadership and responsibility.

'I'm hungry,' he said to the room at large and walked outside. 'Accompany Prakash to his desk and take all office things from him,' he said to the guard. 'Tell Accounts to bring all his papers to me.'

Once Prakash had been herded off by the guard, Tanya, Mumu and I also trooped outside.

'You were great!' I told Mumu. 'That must have taken a lot of work.'

'More genius than work,' said Mumu and smiled, not very modestly.

'I sure got a scare when I walked past that closet and heard Mumu's screams,' said Tanya.

'That's my *dupatta* you conveniently forgot to return,' I told her peevishly.

'I was just walking over to the kitchen after I'd submitted

my papers to Subbu,' continued Tanya without paying the least attention to me, 'to say hello to my old friends, when I heard muffled screams from the closet. Not one to hesitate over any decision...'

'More's the pity,' I muttered.

'...I immediately slammed open the door with my right foot,' she continued. 'In fact, I think I broke the heel of my shoe there.' She held up her right foot for inspection. Mumu appeared most impressed.

'Why didn't you just open it normally, with your hand?' I asked, curiously. 'The door was clearly not latched from the inside.'

'The thought never crossed my mind,' she said after thinking for a moment. 'I have never seen any brave and honest police officer open a door with his or her hand.'

Mumu and I admitted that that was indeed the case. Mumu spoke up at this point. 'If you hadn't come in time, we could not have overpowered Prakash,' she said. 'I was holding on to his shirt for all I was worth but he was unbuttoning at a furious pace. Another minute and I would have been left holding his shirt while he ran free.'

'But Mumu, you should have asked someone to help. You could have called me,' I said.

'Yes, except that you were too busy getting fired. As soon as you went inside to get your dose of poison from the Bat, Prakash slipped out and started to make his way in the direction of the basement. When I saw this, I immediately knew that he considered himself safe for a few minutes and would proceed to do whatever he did in that closet. I knew that this was my chance to catch him red-handed and I followed him, in my usual feline fashion,' explained Mumu.

I groaned and quickly disguised it under a hacking cough.

'And I was right,' Mumu went on. 'Prakash started to take a used laptop out, probably to ship it to a buyer, when I barged in and told him that his game was up and he stood, in fact, discovered. Prakash panicked when he saw that I not only knew what he did but also had evidence to support my claim. He tried to make a run for it but you know me...'

'Yes, all feline grace,' I completed her words.

'Yes,' she agreed with a vehement nod. 'I grabbed his shirt and started screaming for help.'

'I'm so glad I landed there at just the right moment,' Tanya said with a shudder. 'Imagine if Mumu had been subjected to a view of his hairless chest! I kicked him hard and he fell down. Then I helped Mumu sit on him and twist his arm behind him and then ran for help.'

We had reached the office floor. Mumu went inside the Bat's office to ask for further instructions. I went dolefully to my desk to collect my things. Lardie and Varun were sitting together yet again. Lardie was wearing a purple number. She saw me and picked up something to show me with a familiar smirk. It was a copy of *Azura*. I winced and did not say anything, deciding that poisoning the water supply to her house was the only suitable way to avenge myself. Varun and she giggled, decidedly having a good time over my misfortune. Mumu came rushing to me.

'We've all been called inside for a debriefing,' she said. 'Come on!'

'Alright,' I said. 'I'll be right there.'

'What debriefing?' called out Lardie from her perch. 'You don't even work here anymore. You should hand over everything to me.'

'Well, as it happens,' I said over my shoulder, 'there's a lot that happens in this office that you don't know about. In fact, come to think of it, that's equally true of the people you hang out with.'

'What does that mean?' said Lardie and got up to rush to my side. 'What do you know that I don't? I am coming along to Avinash's office right now. Varun, you come too. God only knows what she has told Avinash about us.'

'Suit yourself,' I said and walked to Avinash's office. To my surprise, Tanya was already sitting there.

'I was called too,' she whispered to me. Mumu stood in one corner. Avinash finished talking on the phone and narrowed his eyes when he saw Lardie and Varun.

'What?' he asked a pertinent question.

'Sir, I assume I will be taking over Mini's responsibilities,' started Lardie, 'so I came to ask...'

'Hm mmm,' said Avinash. I hung my head down like a Labrador caught with its front paws in the cookie jar.

'Actually, after the events of today,' said Avinash. 'I may or may not need to consider some of my decisions.' I looked up hopefully.

'So Mumu first,' he said. 'A job well done. We might say that we appreciate your bravery.'

Mumu looked like she had stuffed her mouth with rasgullas,

a decidedly pleasant situation to be in but one that renders speech impossible.

The rest of us stared at each other in complete disbelief. The Bat had uttered words that sounded like 'job well done' and 'appreciation'. Next we would see flying objects rain down gold on the city.

'Now that that bastard Prakash will not be working with us anymore, I would like you to take his place with immediate effect,' he said.

Mumu did not know whether this was good news or not. She seemed to make some swift mental calculations.

'So I am now the chief aide to the CEO,' she asked, a little uncertainly.

'Yes, yes, you have to be quicker than that,' Avinash said waving his hands impatiently. 'You will get a big raise going by the scraps you were earning as the assistant and all sorts of other perks that you can check with John Peters — why haven't we replaced him yet?'

Mumu stared at him.

'I don't know,' she offered.

'Then what sort of a no-good chief aide are you anyway?' barked Avinash. 'Go and find a sodding HR person, will you?'

Mumu got up and scurried off, a bewildered expression on her face.

'You!' he looked at Tanya.

'Tanya,' Tanya said comfortably, not an employee and gleeful about it.

'Whatever, you can join back,' said Avinash, looking like

every word was causing him acute pain in the belly. 'You were ... brave too.'

'Of course I was brave,' Tanya addressed the gathering and suddenly held up her right foot again. 'Look at my shoe! I broke the heel getting the door open.'

Lardie had probably swallowed a frog whole, going by her expression. Varun looked as if he wanted to be far, far away from this end chapter setting.

'Well, whatever,' said Avinash. 'So will you be coming back from tomorrow? You can join Shipra's team given that Mini will be leaving, though of course I am yet to make up my mind about that.' Lardie gasped with horror at this. This was bizarre — Tanya replacing me. I almost laughed aloud at the turn things were taking.

'That won't be necessary,' said Tanya, holding out her hand and suddenly dipped her hand in her pocket to take out something.

'My cards,' she said. 'Please do think of me the next time you have a wedding in the family. Or even your own.'

Avinash looked stunned. He picked up a card.

'Why is this girl sitting under an umbrella,' he asked, confused.

'Oh that's me,' said Tanya. 'This was the defining moment in my corporate life that really spurred me to kick all of this,' here she waved her arms about, 'and do things that really matter. By the way, I will branch out into baby showers soon.'

Avinash shook his head and got up.

'So you will not come back then,' he surmised.

'Nope!' said Tanya. 'Oh dear, I do hope I've not upset you. This is ironical. I was right there in your basement all this while, banished by your orders from life upstairs and now that you do want me back up, I'd rather not. Such is life and all that. I will take your leave now.'

'Shit,' said Avinash after Tanya had gone out. 'I didn't know she sat in the basement. Who put her there anyway?'

The three of us kept silent.

'Now, you, Mini,' said Avinash. 'As we all know, you have made a royal hash of things. The *Azura* cover is...'

At this moment, the *Azura* cover walked inside. After we had got over this surreal experience, we realised that it was actually Anuradha Menon who had walked in and was currently in the process of cooing at Avinash.

'Oh baby,' she simpered. 'Did I disturb you?'

'Haw haw, not at all,' said Avinash, looking very disturbed.

'I just saw the cover and I wanted to ask you if you thought I looked nice,' she said and plonked herself on his lap, twinkling at all of us.

'Yes, yes,' said Avinash hastily. 'Err, can all of you come back later?'

'Baybee,' said Anuradha, getting up and taking a chair on the other side of the room. 'I am sitting right here, in my little corner. Why don't you just finish with all these people and then we can go out for lunch?'

Avinash stared miserably at her. Clearly Anuradha had worked her magic on the man in the time that had passed between the cover shoot and now.

'What, hon?' she prodded. He nodded.

'Yes, dear, we will just wrap this up as quickly as we can then,' he said, and I beamed with joy at how effectively Anuradha had pecked this horrible mass of manhood into kowtowing to her wishes. At least some good had come out of this pile of garbage that I had created.

'So as I was saying,' Avinash went back into raging monster mode once Anuradha has settled in her chair and picked up the magazine lying on the table. 'You, this has been terrible! Disastrous! Even with your talent for messing things up. What were you thinking?'

I let my head hang in the way that it was used to.

'Darling! What are you calling a disaster?' piped up Anuradha from her corner.

'The cover, Anu, what else?' said Avinash. 'My logo is missing and my brand has been misspelt. It doesn't get worse than this. I will now have to hire a team of external morons who will need to assess the damage to the brand and the associated cost implications to explain to the Board. I don't need extra expenses! I have enough expenses! Why should I have to incur extra expenses?'

'Do you really think that the cover is a disaster, Avinash?' Anuradha asked and all the water in the room turned to ice. Everyone turned to look at her. An eyebrow was arched and a faint sneer formed around her lips. Alarm bells started ringing inside Avinash's skull and he looked at her with trepidation.

'What, darling?' he asked.

'I asked, do you really think that the cover is a disaster?' she said as the room continued to steadily turn into the Tundra region.

'No, no, that is not what I meant. In fact, you look fabulous, dear, you always do,' he fumbled. 'I am only talking about the brand and the damage that has been done to the...'

'So you can actually see the damage beyond my flawless skin and my gorgeous hair?' asked Anuradha. 'All this logo nonsense still matters, does it?' Lardie, Varun and I decided to become invisible for as long as it took for Avinash to crawl out of this situation.

'Err, of course not, dear, but I am the CEO, you know,' he said, realising that his romantic life was in grave danger now. Anuradha stood up and tossed back her mane of lustrous hair. Her eyes became steely and glinty, not quite a pleasant sight to behold. Avinash visibly quivered in his Ferragamo shoes.

'So you think you can call a cover on which I have appeared disastrous?' thundered Anuradha.

'I'm just discussing something with the team that handles the brand,' he said pleadingly.

'*Handled* the brand,' said Lardie, unable to contain the joy in her voice. 'She's out of a job anyway.'

'Shut up and speak only when spoken to,' snarled Avinash. Lardie immediately went back to being invisible.

'You have fired Mini!' asked Anuradha. 'For getting me on the cover?'

'Not for getting you on the cover, dear,' Avinash tried to calm the raging inferno in front of him. 'For messing up the logo and the brand.'

'It's the same thing,' said Anuradha.

'Uh, well, it's not the *same...*' Avinash started to say but petered out when he noted that things would not proceed in a direction that would be entirely in his favour if he did.

'May I take your leave now?' I let a few words float in the air. No one paid any attention to me. Clearly it had ceased to be about me a few minutes back.

'Look, Anuradha, why don't you just let me handle all this and go and buy a new bag or something,' Avinash tried to buy his way out of the mess.

'A new bag?' she seethed. 'A new bag? What am I? Some starry-eyed new starlet who you can shut up with a bag? I have bags. Many bags. Bags!'

I had visions of Avinash strangling a starry-eyed new starlet with a bag but wisely kept it to myself.

'No, no, dear, that's not what I meant,' Avinash was in a bad, bad place.

'Well then, you are not firing her. The cover is fine. Perfect, in fact, isn't it, guys?' she turned to us. Lardie and Varun nodded weakly, and I furiously.

Avinash did not have to worry about whether to throw me out or not. Hell, I did not have to worry about where the next month's rent was coming from. The goddess had taken care of me.

'Well then, I guess this is it. Mini, you will stay,' said Avinash in a defeated voice. I decided that this was the time to get noticed.

'Yes sir, thank you sir, I have something to ask of you, sir,' I said.

Avinash nodded.

'I think I may have gained a lot from being under the tutelage of Shipra but I really think that my growth in this role has come to an end, sir. If you know what I mean, sir,' I said and proceeded to bate my breath for his response.

'Is that so, Shipra?' Avinash turned to Lardie.

Lardie sneered in my direction.

'She has been of limited use to me,' she said. 'Take her away, let her be, I couldn't care less.' I gave a small, involuntary whoop of resentment and considered picking up the large, stone Laughing Buddha decorating a corner of the office and flinging it across the room. Perhaps it would home-in on a worthy target along the way?

'Who needs an assistant with more attitude than skill anyway?' she said. Varun nodded vehemently, hanging on to every word that Her Lardness was spewing.

Anuradha stomped her foot loudly, distressed that attention had been diverted from her.

'You can't fire her,' she repeated. 'There's nothing wrong with the cover. I look great. Exquisite, in fact.'

Avinash sighed.

'Anu, I am not firing her anymore. I am just trying to align...' he attempted one last time.

Anuradha responded by flashing him another look. Avinash surrendered arms and decided to call a truce.

'Fine, fine, fine. You!' he said and turned to me. 'You can work on the launch of the new brand. Someone will brief you about that. Now just clear out, will you? All of you! Out! I have a bloody headache. So much nonsense in one day. Out!'

All three of us hastened to clear out. Anuradha crossed the room to sit next to Avinash. As she passed me, she gave me a small wink.

*Huh*, I thought to myself as I got out, *why did she do that?* Anyway, I needed to go and tell Tanya the fabulous news. Then I realised that Lardie was blocking my path, glaring at me with her small, beady eyes.

We were not done yet. No sir, not by a long way.

# *fifteen*

'Oh hello there, old thing,' I said and tried to brush past, a task rendered impossible by her sheer girth.

'Let's go, Ships,' Varun implored.

'Just a minute,' she said imperiously over her shoulder.

'So you think you have managed to pull a coup, eh?' she demanded of me.

'Well, yeah, sort of,' I replied. 'Considering that you left no stone unturned in trying to get me kicked out, I think I did just fine.'

She circled around me like a devotee performing a *parikrama* around a temple or a vulture waiting for meal-time, the latter being slightly more appropriate as similes go.

'I suggest you continue being careful,' she said, still circling. Tanya came in at this point. I looked at her with pleading eyes, asking her silently to rescue me. She gave me a thumbs-up and fled the scene.

'Alright, I will be careful,' I said, trying to dismiss her. 'Why don't you focus on Varun instead? He looks like he is missing a girl.'

'Keep Varun out of this,' she hissed at me. 'I am warning you.'

I sighed.

'Will you stop going round and round? You are making me dizzy,' I said. 'I don't want your stupid Varun. He's just a lowly cheat and I don't fraternise with such men. Now clear off, will you?'

'Stop calling me that,' shouted Varun, finally finding his voice.

Tanya rushed back in, dragging a very pale-looking Subbu behind her.

'He saw you at the theatre,' she said. 'Tell them, Subbu!'

'Well, that is true,' said Subbu, adjusting his tie. 'I did have the pleasure of seeing you at the theatre, did I not, Mr Varun? My cousin Sumita informed me that she and your lady friend are both part of the same troupe. That is very nice, I must say. She is very talented. Everyone says that she is going to be the next star once this play becomes a success. You must be very proud, yes?'

Lardie turned to Varun. This seemed to be a good day for women turning into viragos.

'What the hell is he talking about,' she asked in a cold voice, waving a finger in Subbu's direction. 'I thought there was no girlfriend.'

'Mumu followed him, they kissed!' shouted Tanya. 'He is a liar!' Varun turned even paler than he already was.

'Is she telling the truth, Varun?' asked Lardie again. 'Why didn't you tell me?

Varun looked wildly from one woman to the other.

'I didn't say anything because I am not supposed to,' he said and broke down completely, loud sobs suddenly wracking his slim frame. 'I am just a nobody and my girlfriend is a star. Or about to be one, at any rate. It's not about me not wanting to accept her in public. *She* refuses to acknowledge *me*!'

Uh oh. Tanya and I looked at each other. Subbu coughed uncomfortably and slipped out, making some noises about urgently needing to look into some books.

'What do you mean?' asked Lardie, looking as confused as we were feeling.

'She thinks it'll be better to appear single if she becomes a top actress,' said Varun, wiping his eyes with the back of his sleeve, 'and she has threatened to break up with me if anyone gets to know that we are seeing each other.'

'Well, that still doesn't entitle you to be unfaithful to her,' said Tanya.

'I just wanted to make her jealous,' he said. 'I had no idea that I would develop feelings for Mini.'

'Gah,' I said.

'Feelings for … *Mini*?' thundered Lardie as she went into convulsions of rage.

'Well, it didn't last too long,' Varun tried to explain. 'Once Mini told me that she and her friends were responsible for spiking my juice and even following me, I fell out of love with her.'

'Out of *love*?' echoed Lardie, much like an alpine echo good at its work. This was going to be difficult to clean up later.

'But now, it's all over,' said Varun miserably. 'My girlfriend has kicked me out since she found out she was being signed for the lead role in a film and there's no Mini either. I am all yours, Shipra!' he said and coyly extended a hand. Shipra stared at it for a moment and then slapped it soundly. Varun withdrew it with a yelp of pain.

'Who the hell do you think you are,' she screamed, 'coming to me after half the female race has rejected you!'

'I didn't know that it would be a problem with you,' said Varun. This was the worst thing he could have said, as he soon found out. Lardie started looking for things to throw at him. She picked up a thick notebook from Mumu's desk and flung it at him. It missed him narrowly but he quickly reached the understanding that his luck would not last long and started to run, specially since Mumu also kept a large vase on her desk.

'You bloody cad!' Lardie said and gave chase. Tanya and I stared after them.

'Well, that's it, I guess,' I said. Tanya nodded.

'My job here is done. I'm leaving now,' she said. 'Can we meet at the pub in the evening?' I agreed to do so and went to my desk. I sat down and ordered some tea from the canteen. The message light on my cell phone was flashing. I pressed the button to read the message. It was from Rohan.

*Hey you. You're not taking calls right now so I figure you must still be thrashing it out with your boss. I hope Anuradha reached in time and managed things well. See you soon, I hope.*

Huh? How did he know that Anuradha was planning to come to meet Avinash? Did Anuradha plan all this beforehand? Why would she do that? Questions were buzzing like bees all over my already overtaxed brain. I dialled Rohan's number. He picked it up on the first ring.

'Hello, Mini?' he asked, sounding a little breathless.

'Yeah, it's me. Listen, I got the most perplexing message from you,' I said. 'What the hell does it mean anyway?'

'How did things go?' he asked in turn.

'Pretty good, thanks to Anuradha,' I said. 'Did you talk to her?'

'Yes, I did,' he said. 'I spoke to her as soon as I saw the cover and realised that there was a goof-up. Someone would have to hang for that and that would have to be you, going purely by the pecking order.'

'Um yes,' I agreed and then laughed. 'So what exactly did you do?'

'Well, I remembered that your boss had taken a huge fancy for Anuradha during the cover shoot. I called her to ask and she confirmed that they were something of a number since then, which if I know Anuradha at all, means that he has the status of a galley slave in the relationship.'

'That was quite an insight,' I commented.

'Hmm, yes, I *am* pretty insightful that way,' he laughed. 'Anyway, I reminded Anuradha how lovely I can make her cheekbones look and how I'll be shooting several prestigious campaigns this year and let's just say she agreed to go and have a little word with her beau.'

'A barrage of words,' I said. 'You should have seen her! She took him down like a house of cards.'

'Is that so? Well, I'm heartened,' he said and I could hear his grin coming through on the phone.

'Anyway, so the net result was that I did not get fired,' I said, 'and now that I know that I owe it all to you, I want to say thank you.'

'No need,' he said, suddenly gruff. 'I would have done it for anyone else.'

'Then you must be nicer than I ever gave you credit for,' I said.

'Um hum,' he said. 'Anyway, what else is new?'

'There's a ton of office gossip that I can give you. Hey, I'm meeting Tanya and Pri down at Friends and Foes this evening. Why don't you join in?'

'Really? You don't think I'm too old for your crowd?' he asked with a laugh.

'You are, but I think they can organise a wheelchair,' I said and hung up.

I drank the tea that had been deposited at my table and went over the incidents of the day in my mind. It appeared impossible that just this morning I had picked up a copy of *Azura* on my way to work. Since then I had been fired, helped capture a corporate criminal, been rehired, and got Lardie off my back. I took a peek at her desk at this point. She was still not back. I figured she must be chasing Varun off the face of the earth. Yes, life was good indeed. In this new phase of my life, a new brand would be launched and I would be responsible for it. Things would go all over the place, most of them upside down and definitely not as per my plans, but in the end, it would turn out to be alright.

When the evening rolled around, I was still feeling quite optimistic and dressed up in bright colours and even slapped on some make-up.

'Why are you all dressy for us?' asked Tanya as soon as she saw me. Pri whistled softly and swirled the little umbrella in his drink.

'Well, it's not for you, kids,' I said as I settled in and signalled the waiter for my usual. 'It's a symbol of my bright future.'

I told them about my conversation with Rohan.

'Imagine, if he had not pulled strings at the right time, I could have well been on the dole by now,' I said. 'In fact, I asked him to trot along for a drink.'

'Oh, oh, oh, so you've dressed up for him,' exclaimed Tanya. I looked at Pri in exasperation. He grinned at me and said nothing.

'Stop it, you guys. Rohan's old. He ... he is like...' I started.

'Thirty-six,' said Rohan from above my head. 'I'm planning to apply for my senior citizen card next year.'

I turned an unbecoming shade of crimson.

'Stop coming in when I am not expecting you,' I said as I slid over and made place for him. To my intense surprise, he plonked some flowers in my lap.

'Gwa hah,' he said.

'What?' I sought clarification.

'I said, for you,' he said loudly.

'Pri,' I said to my friend who looked like a cat who had just swallowed a carton of fresh cream. 'I'm sure Tanya has aching ribs by now, can you stop nudging her?'

'I know!' exploded Tanya, relieved that she could express herself freely once again. 'Stop poking me with that darned elbow of yours.'

'Thank you for the flowers,' I turned to Rohan who looked away into the distance. 'Though you really shouldn't have.'

Prithvi removed his elbow and rested his chin on his hands, still looking very happy.

'One large rum and coke,' Rohan barked at a passing waiter and ate some complimentary masala peanuts, one of the shining attractions of Friends and Foes.

'You look nervous,' accused Tanya. 'Have you got something to say to Mini? Should we clear out?'

'No! I mean, yes, I do have something to say to her,' stammered Rohan under her piercing gaze, 'and no, you don't have to clear off. I mean, you can go but Prithvi can't.'

'What?' said Tanya, most displeased and then turned to Prithvi. 'What, what, what?'

'Uff, nothing,' he said and tried to put an arm around Tanya which she immediately shrugged off.

'Proceed, dear friend,' he told Rohan.

'So the thing is, Mini,' said Rohan and cleared his throat and continued to look into the distance. 'This day is as good as it's going to get.'

I agreed that could well be the case.

'Of course, one could easily argue for the opposite which is to say that tomorrow may be a better day. Than today, I mean,' he carried on.

I acknowledged that the possibility could not be denied.

'But the thing is that one has no way of knowing that with any certainty and therefore one might as well do today what one was in fact planning to delay till tomorrow. Sometimes, even day after tomorrow,' he was still addressing the invisible crowds at the far end of the pub.

'What the hell,' burst Tanya. 'Get on with it, man.'

'I am, I am,' he replied nervously. 'So what do you think, Mini? Do you think it's doable?'

'Huh?' I said, not knowing what had been asked.

'For God's sake, Rohan,' said Prithvi. 'You're terrible! Remember what I told you, shoulders straight and chin up.'

'Wait a minute,' said the ever-perceptive Tanya. 'Have you two been plotting about this ... how should I put it, terribly articulate and blatantly romantic proposal behind our backs?'

Prithvi sighed.

'Plotting is what you do, my dear,' he said. 'All we did was just discuss the best strategy for conducting these negotiations.'

He turned to Rohan who was now perspiring profusely.

'Go for it again, man,' he encouraged.

Rohan nodded and turned to me.

'Huh, what, huh?' he asked.

Prithvi groaned and I held out my hand to silence any recriminations and turned to address Rohan.

'I get it,' I said. 'But *dude*!'

'I'd like to ask you out,' he finally exploded.

'I gathered but I had no idea.'

'I'm telling you now.'

'I heard, I heard.'

'So what do you say, eh?'

'Your drink is here.'

'I know.'

Gulp.

'Can I have a repeat, please?'

'Yes, sir.'

'You haven't replied.'

'I'm still thinking.'

'Don't you like me even a little bit?'

'I like you a lot but you're asking for a tad more than that.'

'Yeah, I guess I am. I thought we could sort of go out, you know?'

'So let me think.'

'Have you thunk?'

'Well, you were very nice to me.'

'I was.'

'And you did everything to make my life easier.'

'I did.'

'I thought you were being sweet.'

'I was.'

'But you felt a little more than just congenial.'

'I did.'

'You are fun and kind.'

'I hope so.'

'You are somewhat older.'

'I am.'

'However, that shouldn't matter.'

'No.'

'So I guess we could see how it goes.'

'Yes, we could.'

'Let's.'

'Yeah!'

Post this exchange of words, there was much cheering and,

thumping of tables and backs and 'get us some drinks here my man's and we all proceeded to dilute our bloodstreams with alcohol. Later that evening, Rohan dropped me home. I dodged past Urvashi's boyfriend who, judging by his peaceful expression, had clearly been inhaling *something*, and went into my bedroom. After I had changed, I lay down on my bed and went over the recent proceedings in my head. What a day it had been. Hell, what a strange few months it had been. Maybe things would be different from now on. Who was to say? I tossed and turned for sometime but there was too much excitement circulating in the system for me to be able to sleep. Finally, I called my father.

'What's wrong?' he sounded wide awake.

'Nothing,' I said.

'Good. What's happening?'

'What's happiness?'

'Happiness is not having a wife who snores.'

'Is that why you're still up?'

'Yes, and because I knew you would call.'

'I nearly got fired today.'

'Nearly?'

'Got saved in the nick of time.'

'Try harder next time.'

'Yes, I think I will have another go at it. '

'Did you at least have fun?

I thought for a moment.

'Well, yes, I guess I did.'

'In that case, it wasn't so bad then, was it?'

I thought for another moment.

'No, it wasn't.'

'If you get fired, you can come here and stay with us.'

'Wouldn't you be ashamed of me?'

'Not if you are toilet-trained.'

'Dad!'

'Seriously, you were the toughest child to toilet-train.'

'And that is why I will not come to your house.'

'Ah, fine, maybe you will find someone else then?'

I kept quiet for a moment.

'Yeah, about that…'

'Take your time to tell us.'

'Um hmm, I'll go now. Later, Daddy.'

He was right. It hadn't been too bad after all.

# Acknowledgments

I'd like to thank some people who made this book come alive.

Sainath, for treating my success and failure as his own. Every time.

Aditya, for bringing a lot of joy to my life and Ragini, for doubling it.

My family, for the pride they take in what I do.

My friends, for their very vocal support.

Deepthi, my wonderful editor at Westland, for answering the questions. There were many.

Madhu, at Landmark, for keeping the faith that first time.

The readers of my blog, for laughing. There is no music sweeter than that.

You all have my gratitude.